QUARRY

www.frosthollowpub.com

First Edition

Text set in Garamond Pro
Copyright 2009 by Robert Holland
Printed on acid-free paper in Canada
ISBN 978-0-9794273-7-4

Cover and Illustrations by
Rick LaMarre

Frost Hollow Publishers,LLC
411 Barlow Cemetery Road
Woodstock, CT 06281
phone: 860-974-2081
fax: 860-974-0813
email: frosthollow@mindspring.com

www.frosthollowpub.com

QUARRY

A Novel of Sports and Mystery
by

ROBERT HOLLAND

To: Lauren
great to meet you — and
thanks for the great questions.
All the best,

[signature]

FROST HOLLOW PUBLISHERS
Woodstock, Connecticut

2009

1... THE QUARRY

The high whining roar of a car engine blasted through the silence, howling as it came closer, and both of us whirled and looked up toward the sixty-foot high cliff on the left hand side of the quarry as a car shot out of the woods and went airborne, slowly pivoting forward, the engine screaming, the wheels spinning. Seconds later it landed upside down in the water and sent what looked like about an eight foot high tidal wave in all directions.

Only when we understood that we were about to get wet did we turn and look for high ground. There wasn't any. We were standing in a big open lot that had once been used as the landing area for the blocks of granite.

"There!" I shouted and Jack and I ran toward a pile of the blocks that had been left behind.

Spurred on by the roar of the wave crashing up over the edge of the quarry behind us, man, did we run. We jumped up onto the first block and then the second and finally the third as the water poured past.

"Cam, that was awesome!" Jack shouted. "Can you believe

what we just saw?"

All I could do was shake my head.

The water, once it hit the flat open area, spread out quickly and no more than a six-inch flood swirled past the blocks where we stood, and even that dissipated quickly as the water, as always, sought its own level. Some ran off into the woods, the rest sank into the sandy soil. I looked out at the car as it nosed down, the water driving the air from the inside in big spurts, the car sinking lower and lower until it slipped beneath the surface.

"Say something, Dude!" Jack said.

I couldn't talk. I didn't have any words to fit what I had just seen. I looked back up toward the top of the cliff where two men in suits stood on the edge, looking down at the water. They turned our way and I grabbed Jack by the arm.

"We gotta get out of here!"

"What?"

I jumped down off the granite blocks, "Just run!" I took off for the woods with Jack right behind. In seconds we had made it into the cover of the trees and I could hear Jack cursing as the branches whipped back at him. For the first time ever, I thought maybe being five-ten had some advantages over being six-three like Jack, because I could get lower more quickly. But I'd also spent a lot more time in the woods. Jack was kind of an open ground guy who favored lawns and paved surfaces.

I spotted a cluster of boulders up ahead and ran that way, getting behind the rocks and pulling Jack down out of sight as I took out my cell phone and punched in nine-one-one, told the dispatcher what we had seen, and closed the phone.

Jack started to talk and I put my hand over his mouth and shook my head. Then we waited and I held my breath so my

Quarry

breathing would not interfere with my hearing as I listened for the sound of someone coming through the woods. Some people can do that without making any noise, but I was guessing that guys in suits weren't in that category.

Then, in the distance, from the direction where the car had gone over the edge, I heard an engine start, followed by the sound of tires spinning on a gravel road, the stones clattering against the underside of the fender wells.

The sound faded quickly and the quiet closed around us. It could be a trick, a way to decoy us out into the open, but I didn't think so. They needed to get away fast, because they had to know that every kid alive had a cell phone and would already have called for help.

"It's okay," I said.

"Good! That's good. I thought I was gonna bust."

I grinned.

"Can you tell me what's going on here?"

"There were two guys in suits standing on the edge of the quarry where the car went over. They got a good look at us and my guess is that what we just saw was a mob hit."

"You mean like in the movies?"

"Only not a movie," I said.

"Which makes us witnesses."

"Yeah."

"And they saw us."

"They did."

"This is not gonna make my mother happy."

"Might be smart not to tell her," I said.

"Smart is a good thing."

"It has its uses."

"Do you think they can identify us?" Jack asked.

"I'm hoping they were too far away."

"Could you identify them?"

"Yeah."

"But you've got that long distance vision thing, and maybe they don't."

"Probably not." I was pretty sure they didn't because according to what I'd read, only about one in a hundred thousand humans can see as well as I can, which is about half as well as a red-tailed hawk.

We walked back down to the edge of the quarry and now, in the distance, I could hear a siren. I looked out at the still water and for the first time I got an idea of how big the place was. My guess was something close to twenty acres, surrounded by sheer cliffs that plunged straight into the water with no shoreline. The only access to the water was where we stood. I turned and looked up at the cliff where the car had gone airborne but from where I stood I could see no sign of what had happened and it was hard to believe we hadn't imagined the whole thing.

"How high is that cliff, you think?"

"Sixty feet or so."

Jack swiveled his baseball cap forward to shade his eyes from the steadily brightening sky. "Would you jump from there?"

"Are you nuts?"

He grinned. "Be a heck of a rush."

"All you have to do is hit the water the wrong way and you could break your neck."

"You think?"

"Even if it didn't kill you, you might break a leg or your back or ... or worse."

Quarry

"Worse? What could be worse?"

I pointed to my crotch.

"Ouch!" Jack said. "I never thought about that."

I took off my hat and rubbed my hand over my sandy buzz cut hair. "Were you really thinking about jumping?"

"Sure."

"Do you know anything about abandoned quarries?"

He shrugged. "You mean beyond the fact that there's nobody here?"

"Duh ..."

"What's to know?"

"A lot, a whole lot," I said.

"Like what?"

"These things are usually full of mining equipment. When they finish they just leave it there because it's too much trouble to haul it back up."

"How far down would it be?"

"It depends ..."

"Yeah, got it. It depends on how deep the quarry is."

"Right."

We heard the siren clearly now.

"Where does the water come from?" Jack asked.

"Dad says it's ground water and springs. He says that in deep quarries they have to keep pumps going all the time so the place doesn't fill up. It's one of the reasons they quit. They can't stay ahead of the water."

"I can't believe how clear the water is," Jack said.

"Look around the edges. There's no shore. The rock just goes straight down. With no sand or mud to get stirred up by the wind, the water stays clear."

"Oh man, if you fell in at the far end you'd have to swim all the way back here to get out."

"That's another problem."

I glanced around at him, dressed as usual in his homey clothes, baggy jeans nearly falling off, sneakers laced but untied. He sure didn't look like a guy from a swim team. I shook my head and looked down at his shoes, wondering how he'd managed to run through the woods without tripping. It seemed almost miraculous.

"We could jump into the water here, swim over, dive down, and see if there's a dead guy in the car," Jack said.

For Jack, who could swim like an otter and float like a cork, it was no big deal. But while I could swim just fine, floating wasn't exactly in my bag of tricks. In fact, I floated about like a large stone.

"We'd need some equipment," I said. "A boat and ropes, lots of ropes, and ..."

"No way, Dude! It's easy."

"Do you remember how cold the water is this time of year? It's not like a pool."

"There's gotta be some way to get down there first," Jack said, "I hate to give up a chance to be famous."

"Famous? You'd risk you life just for fame?"

"Hey, easy for you to say, Dude. But then you're captain of the lacrosse team. All I do is swim and nobody ever comes to our meets."

"You get more than we do at lacrosse."

"No way."

"Anyway, it doesn't matter because you get all the college scouts."

Quarry

"Huh?"

"The colleges. They send scouts."

"Where'd you hear that?"

"At your last meet I met a guy from Ohio State."

"No way ...."

"Those guys are always looking for talent. But he wouldn't tell me who he was there to watch."

He slapped his hand on his thigh. "That is so awesome!"

"Good thing he left before you changed, though."

"What's that supposed to mean?"

"I've been meaning to say something about this for a while now. You gotta lose the prison pants."

"Prison pants?"

"Don't you know that's where the homey look comes from? Guys in prison can't have belts because they might commit suicide. So their pants always hang low. When they get out of prison and come back home they still wear their pants halfway down their butts. It caught on."

"Where do you come up with stuff like this?"

"I read the papers."

"Papers? Oh, man, what century are you living in? Nobody reads papers, they go on the Net."

"The point is, Jack, you gotta change your look. You don't find any homeys on college swimming teams."

"Preppy. They all dress like preppies."

"So if you have to do that to get a full free ride through college, is that a big sacrifice?"

"This is a matter of style, Dude!"

I looked up at him, staring into his blue eyes. "Is it?"

"Man ...." Jack shook his head. "You don't leave a guy much

room, do you?"

"There are two options: win or lose."

"So?"

"Winning is getting the free ride. Losing is not getting it and always wondering why you didn't get it."

"What're people gonna think?"

I shrugged. "Who cares, man? Especially when it comes to clothes. But I'll tell you this. Last year you wouldn't have seen any of the guys on the lacrosse team dressed the way you are. Coach wouldn't have let 'em on the bus."

"No way. He'd do that?"

"He had a dress code."

"You mean like coat and tie?"

I laughed. "No, khakis and polo shirts. He said it was like camouflage. Anyone watching us get off the bus couldn't tell anything about us, except that we looked organized. We looked like a team and not just a bunch of individuals."

"What about at school?"

I looked off over the quarry and then turned and looked back at him. "Who are you trying to impress? The girls?"

"Why not?"

"Think about it."

Down on the road the siren shut off and we could hear the car making its way toward us.

2... Investigating

It didn't take long for the cruiser to appear. The driver spotted us, drove over to where we stood, shut it off, and climbed out. He was tall, maybe six-five, and he had shoulders wider than Jack's, which is saying something because swimmers have serious shoulders. He wore a neatly pressed blue uniform and he looked like a man who was used to uniforms.

Until that moment I had never talked to a cop. I hadn't even thought about it, and the thing is, I was pretty uneasy. Cops arrested people and somehow I had this idea that you could get arrested for pretty much anything. Sure, I knew what was right and wrong, but I wasn't at all clear, for example, on whether we might be trespassing.

"Hi," he said, "you the guys that called in something about a car in the quarry?"

"I did," I said and pointed toward the cliff where the car had come over the edge. "We heard the engine and then it flew off the edge and fell into the water."

He nodded and looked down at the wet ground. He smiled. "Looks like it threw up a pretty good wave."

"About like a tsunami," I said. "We climbed onto that pile of blocks. Then a couple of men in suits came out of the woods and looked down into the water and we took off and hid until they left." I tried to act and sound as if I talked to cops all the time, but I was pretty sure I hadn't fooled him.

He nodded. "Let's go have a look."

I led the way through the brush with the cop behind me and Jack following him.

I stopped at the tire tracks and he saw them and followed them to the edge.

"Well," he said, "looks like we've got a mystery here, all right." He unclipped the radio from his shirt and called back to headquarters for a big wrecker.

He clipped the radio back to his shirt pocket then turned and grinned. "What were you guys doing up here?"

Okay. No lies. Never lie to the police. I had no idea whether that was illegal or not, but it sure seemed like it might be.

"We heard there was an old quarry up here and we wanted to see what it looked like."

He smiled. "Well, who wouldn't?"

"Are we trespassing?" I asked.

"The land isn't posted that I could see." He shook his head. "If you hadn't seen it happen, we'd probably never have known." He looked down into the water. "I hope you guys don't have any ideas about swimming here," he said and this time he looked directly at Jack. "A guy like you, spend half your life in the water, it probably came to mind, huh?"

Jack grinned, surprised that the cop knew who he was. "Cam talked me out of it." He pointed to the edge. "He said his father had told him about quarries being dangerous."

QUARRY

"Well, good for him," he said. "And by the way my name is Tom Kiernan. But just call me Tom."

Okay, it was a "good cop" move, and I've heard about stuff like that before. They make friends and it helps them find out who's doing drugs and who's selling drugs. And here's the thing: that's fine with me. I don't even drink beer. I play lacrosse and I'm going to college and play lacrosse, and stuff like drinking and drugs can take that away from you.

For several minutes Tom looked around, and then he turned and looked down into the quarry again.

"I think this job might prove pretty challenging." He took the mike off his pocket and raised the dispatcher. "Helen, I think you better call in the State Police dive team. It's not gonna be easy getting this car out of here."

He switched off the mike and pointed to the tire tracks. "Let's see where these go."

Where they went was back through the low growing brush, steadily downhill to what remained of an old road. There, he found another set of tire tracks.

"Does that mean what I think it means?" I asked.

"Yup. They came up here in two cars and then sent one off the edge and walked back to the second car."

"You think there's a body in there?" Jack asked. He was looking a little wild-eyed.

Tom nodded. "It happens," he said. Then he grinned. "You sure you guys want to hang around and see this?"

"It'll probably be pretty ugly, won't it?" I asked.

"Most likely," Tom said.

"Wouldn't miss it," I said.

He laughed and clapped me on the shoulder. "Me either, especially when I was your age." He turned toward the tire tracks. "I'm gonna have a look around, see what I can find."

"You mean like evidence?" Jack asked.

"Sometimes the least detail makes the difference."

"Sherlock Holmes," I said.

"Pretty close. You have to make your eyes scan the ground and look for anything that doesn't belong." He pointed several times toward the ground. "But I want you guys to stay right here, until I finish."

"So we don't mess up the crime scene, I mean, if it is a crime scene," I said.

"That's the way I have to treat it for now." He began moving forward a step at a time as he headed toward where the first car had entered and gone up the road. Now and then he squatted to get a better look, brushing the grass with his hand and then standing up and moving on.

The rain from the day before had softened the ground and on the outside of the track, on the driver's side of the car, he stopped and looked closely. Then he looked up at us and waved his hand.

"Cross up there and keep well away from the tracks, I want to show you something."

We did as he had directed.

First he pointed to the ground off to his right. "You see where the grass has been flattened? It looks as if there may have been a body there. There are more footprints and then you can see two lines in the dirt as if they dragged the body to the car." He rubbed his chin. "Com'on, follow me."

We walked out to the main road and then back in, staying well away from the car tracks.

"What we're searching for are cartridge cases." He looked

around at me. "You know what they look like."

I nodded and Jack shook his head. He came from a no-gun family and I'd grown up shooting and hunting.

"The way I figure this, if the guy was shot while he was standing by the car, and if he was shot with an automatic, then the cartridge casings would have flown in this direction. Most likely they would have sailed over the roof of the car and landed about here." He pointed to a very thick patch of grass and weeds.

"Cam, you know what to look for, so you start there and I'll start here." He looked around at me. "If you see one, just tell me, but don't pick it up."

"Fingerprints," I said.

"Not many guys load their guns with gloves on."

"Doesn't the heat destroy the prints?" I asked.

"If there's enough oil in the chamber of the pistol it will sometimes harden and you can see the print without having to dust the metal." He grinned at me. "This grass is pretty thick, so you'll want to check yourself for ticks when you get home."

We began searching and it was a slow, painstaking job, moving through the grass inches at a time. Finding spent cartridge cases can be a pain. When Dad, my brother Lance, and I shoot the forty-fives, we usually spread a big tarp to catch the empties. If they land on their sides in the grass you can spot the bright brass pretty easily, but when they land on the bottom where the primer is, all that shows is the thin, blackened end of the shell, and sometimes you never find them.

Knowing that, we both got down on our hands and knees and spread the grass apart, the low angle giving us a better chance to pick up the glint of brass.

And it did. We found four casings, all bright and shiny and

crawling with fingerprints. Tom picked up each shell by sliding a pencil into the open mouth of it and putting it into a separate plastic bag.

"Spent casings can give us some other information," Tom said. "Every gun chamber is slightly different from another and when the shell expands against the walls of the chamber, those marks get left on the softer brass."

"Awesome," Jack said.

"Cam, what's your guess, looking at these shells, did the bullets pass through the victim?"

"A forty-five, at close range, they'd have to go through unless they were some kind of target load."

"Which means what?"

Not only did I shoot a lot, but I loved crime shows. "We might find a bullet in a nearby tree that we could dig out for the ballistics guys."

He laughed. "You are good!" he said. "Almost as good as you are on the field."

"You've seen our games?"

"Sure."

"Why would you do that?"

He shrugged. "I keep track of things."

"That'll work," I said.

He watched me carefully for several seconds and nodded.

I knew what he was keeping track of. Up until now there had been trouble over marijuana and some prescription stuff but suddenly there were other drugs around. What Tom meant to do was stamp it out fast, and that wasn't gonna hurt my feelings.

About then another cruiser pulled up and Tom walked down and directed the officer to the quarry road while we checked the

QUARRY

trees for a bullet mark. You might think that the chances were pretty slim, but you'd be wrong. A bullet fired into even a small woodlot never comes out the other side. Look at it this way. If you took all the trees in that lot and pulled them into a row no wider than ten feet, you'd have a solid wall of trees.

Doesn't mean though, that in that ten-acre patch you'll find which tree a bullet hit. We improved our odds by making a guess about the probable line of travel, based on the impression the body had left in the grass, and then walked back and forth looking at every tree before taking a step forward and repeating the process.

About twenty feet in, I spotted a white hole in the dark bark of a small oak where the bullet had burst through and splintered the wood inside.

When Tom came back, he took out a stout, nasty looking boot knife and dug the bullet from the tree, being careful not to damage the grooves left on it by the rifling in the barrel of the gun. He dropped it into another plastic bag and we walked back to the landing. Things were getting busy.

3 ... From the Depths

Two more cruisers had arrived along with an enormous wrecker. Then came a blue van and a one-ton, four-wheel-drive pickup towing a very large rubber boat, all of which said "State Police Dive Team" on the sides.

Tom introduced us to the other two officers and asked them to put up some crime scene tape out at the road that led up to the cliff and to stop anyone from coming in who had no business here. We walked over to where the wrecker and the dive crew had parked.

Once again we went through a round of introductions and then Tom led them up to the cliff where they could look down through the clear water to the car.

Wilky Hulm, the wrecker driver, a guy with a three-day growth of gray whiskers, a cold cigar butt clamped between his teeth, a pretty large stomach hanging down over his belt, and wearing a greasy shirt, pants, and boots, shook his head and pushed back his greasy baseball cap to display a tangled mass of gray hair.

"Nasty," he said. "The car's sitting on a ledge. If we pull it off the ledge it's gonna drop to the bottom and I got no idea how deep it is." He pointed off to his wrecker, which, by the way, was by far the biggest wrecker I'd ever seen. It looked like a tractor-trailer cab with a wrecker on the back.

"I could pay out cable," Mr. Hulm said, "but the thing is, there's cables running every which-a-ways down there and if the car gets snagged we'll never get it up."

The head of the dive team, Rich Upton, nodded. "Is the wrecker powerful enough to pull the car through the water without it sinking?"

Mr. Hulm rubbed his whiskery chin. "Never tried it." He looked down through the water. "What kinda car is it?"

"We'll have to take a look," Mr. Upton said. "I saw this done on a sunken barge once with an ocean-going tug. They rigged two tow cables in a Y and hooked them to the front underside of the barge."

"So it pulled the bow up," Mr. Hulm said.

"And then they revved up the tug and cut in the power so it started forward with a surge." He grinned. "We'd rigged big inflatables and as soon as the barge broke from the bottom, we set off the charges and that helped bring the bow up more quickly. About ten feet from the surface we set off the big inflatables inside the hull and up she came."

Mr. Hulm grinned. "Like to have seen that. Them tugs is powerful, got them big turbo diesels."

Mr. Upton grinned. "It was awesome!"

"Won't need quite that much gear," Mr. Hulm said.

Mr. Upton nodded. "All we have to do is keep the front of the car up so the bottom acts like a boat hull until we get it into shallow water." He looked down at the car. "We can't put an inflatable inside the car because there might be a body in there and we can't risk damaging it." He grinned. "A thing like that gives the forensics guys wedgies."

Mr. Hulm pointed back to the flat area where the trucks were parked. "Tricky part will be hauling it up and over that edge." He rubbed his chin some and then massaged the back of his neck and finally he pulled the brim of his hat down, a signal he was ready to start working. "I'll get the wrecker rigged."

It took about a half-hour before the four-man team had loaded all their gear into the large rubber raft, motored out, and moored the raft where it wouldn't run afoul of any other lines. One of the coolest things was a small generator that powered a set of hydraulic metal cutters.

I suppose there are people who would find stuff like this boring, but that isn't me. We're talking machines and tools, and stuff like that is awesome. My dad understands. He manages his hedge fund five days a week and the rest of the time, along with my younger brother, Lance, we build stuff and tear down old engines and hunt and fish, which includes loading all our own ammo and tying flies and making our own lures.

When you live in a town that borders the Connecticut River, and you've got a fast boat, you can always find fish to chase, everything from great northern pike to the striped bass and shad that come up from the salt water, not to mention the sea-run trout.

But just then my head was bursting with questions and all I could do was watch and record everything I saw. What kind of surprised me was that Jack, who doesn't do any of that kind of stuff, was equally fascinated.

"This is so cool," he said. "Did you see that big set of cutters? It looks like something your dad would have."

QUARRY

"Did you ever think about taking up diving?" I asked.

He shook his head. "Not until now."

We watched the divers drop over the side of the raft and disappear. Mr. Hulm backed his wrecker up to about ten feet from the edge of the quarry, pulled a heavy, y-shaped cable from one of the boxes on the side, and laid it out for the divers.

My dad is big on details. He's always saying things like "the devil is in the details" and telling us that if we want to understand what we're seeing, we need to see what we're seeing. When I was younger that didn't make any sense. And then one day, it did. Go figure. What I most wanted to watch were the divers.

Jack poked me with one of his bony elbows and it reminded me of the days when he had played lacrosse with me in the summer club league. We were on opposite teams and he was the point man on offense and I played defense. When he carried the ball, he guarded it with those nasty sharp elbows.

"Hey," he said, "let's go watch them."

We ran up to where we could see down into the water.

The sun had climbed higher by then and I was amazed at how far down we could see. I was even more amazed by what we saw. Cars: maybe ten or more, resting on the bottom, perhaps another fifty feet below the ledge. And suddenly I got this really creepy feeling. What if there were bodies in all those cars? What did that mean? Was this some kind of mafia burial ground? I'd heard about things like that on the news.

Tom had followed us and now he saw the cars too. "Not good," he said. "Not good at all. We're gonna be hauling cars out of here for a week."

"Do you think anyone's in 'em?" I asked.

"Hard to say," he said. "Just be a guess. But if there's a body in the first one then the odds go up there'll be more. We could solve a whole lot of missing persons cases here."

We watched the divers cut away several cables and then they surfaced and ran the boat back to get the cable from the wrecker. They used two really big floats to keep the cable from sinking and threaded the cable through rings in the bottom of each float so the cable could run free and give them enough slack to reach the car.

They handed Mr. Hulm a set of earphones attached to a long black cord, and then towed the rig back out, unreeling the communication cable as they went. I understood. They had to let the cable down slowly and stop it at the right point and that meant Mr. Hulm had to know how fast to pay out the cable.

It was tricky work but they took their time and then finally dropped down to the car and hooked on the two ends of the Y-shaped cable. Mr. Hulm climbed into the wrecker, put it in gear, and slowly took the slack out of the cable, which pulled the two big floats below the surface.

I'm not sure what I had expected, but certainly a lot more than I saw. Once he had the cable taut, he gunned the big engine in the truck, shifted gears on the winch and then shifted the winch into high gear and it never hesitated, reeling in the big steel fish on the end of the line.

In no more than a minute the car broke the surface of the water and headed for shore, picking up speed and throwing a huge bow wave. Where the water shallowed out near the edge of the quarry, Mr. Hulm slowed the winch until the car settled onto the flat rock and then he pulled it along so slowly it looked as if the car were driving itself.

At about six feet from the edge, the angle of the cable changed

QUARRY

so that now the winch drew the front of the car up out of the water until only the back wheels touched the bottom. He shifted the wrecker into an extra low gear and crept forward, drawing the car closer, until it touched the lip of the quarry and then he activated the winch from inside the cab and pulled the car higher and higher, even as the wrecker moved forward at snail speed. When the car reached the point where there was more weight over ground than there was in the water, it simply tipped forward onto its front wheels and Mr. Hulm drew it up until it sat on all four wheels.

Water poured out of every crevice, and Tom walked over and pulled open the passenger side door and jumped out of the way as the water gushed out. When it had slowed to a trickle, Tom walked over and looked into the car, shook his head, and stepped back. He unclipped the radio mike and raised headquarters for what he called a "meat wagon".

We started to edge closer but he stopped us. "You might not want to look at what's in there," he said. "Kinda ugly."

"Is it a body?" Jack asked.

He nodded. "No need to look." He shook his head. "But I'm guessing you have to, right?"

We both nodded.

He shook his head. "Go ahead but if you're gonna throw up, do it over there. I can't stand that smell."

So we looked and he was right. It was ugly. The guy had been shot at least twice in the head and then in the chest and the holes were still oozing blood. But there was no odor and I thought maybe that's because it had been underwater. It looked like something had been chewing on the face.

"Something's been eating it!" Jack said.

"Probably crayfish," Tom said.

"Whoa ... crayfish," I said. "Bass bait eats people?"

"Scavengers," Tom said. "To them this is nothing more than a giant free lunch."

"And that makes me think maybe I don't wanna eat any more bass," Jack said.

I laughed. Jack had an appetite like a bear getting ready to hibernate. "Hey, no worry, Dude," I said. "By the time you get it the meat is bass meat. First the crayfish eat it and it becomes crayfish meat and then the bass eat the crayfish and it becomes ..."

"Whoa, whoa," he said. "Way too much information. I don't want stuff like that coming between me and my food."

I kept on looking at the distorted face, trying to imagine what it had once looked like but it didn't work.

We heard the engine start on the big rubber boat and watched the divers head to shore. I backed away from the car, having seen as much as I needed and, to tell you the truth, feeling a little queasy.

The divers secured their boat and walked over to where we stood near the car.

"There's a lot more cars down there," Mr. Upton said. "I counted eighteen. We'll have to haul every one of them. They're in eighty feet of water, but it shouldn't be a problem because they're on the bottom and it's a smooth incline all the way." He nodded toward the car.

"Anything in 'em?" Tom asked.

Mr. Upton glanced at us and then nodded. "Every one," he said.

Tom nodded. "Then we need to pull them out." He paused. "This needs to be done right."

QUARRY

Mr. Upton grinned. "So when the feds take over the case they don't blame you when they can't solve it."

"Every time I get an interesting case, either your guys or the feds move in and I'm back to writing traffic tickets."

"I told you to become a trooper," Mr. Upton said.

"Yeah, I know."

"Then why not?"

"Too much bureaucracy."

"There's that all right. It'll take me a day to fill out the paperwork from this one car." He laughed. "The more we find, the more paperwork we'll have to fill out. And I gotta tell you, Tom, I never saw so many bodies in one place before. Even down in Portland we found only a couple of bodies and those quarries are a lot bigger."

We hung around and the state police forensic team arrived in their "meat wagon" and we watched them bag the body. They were loading it into the van when an unmarked car pulled up and two men, wearing suits, climbed out and walked over to us. Clearly, the state was taking over and I felt bad for Tom. It only seemed fair that he have a chance to solve the case, but then maybe he hadn't gotten the right training. That meant education, too, and the one thing I knew absolutely was that to go anywhere you had to have knowledge and training.

"So," the shorter of the two guys said. "Somebody give me some information."

I watched the divers turn away and go about their business, pointedly refusing to talk to him.

Tom grinned and told him what had happened.

The man listened but his eyes and the way he moved displayed nothing but contempt for a local police officer. While he listened, the younger man with him took notes.

"We'll need something in writing," he said to Tom.

"Expected you would," Tom said. "Give me a card."

The guy reached into his pocket and took out a small leather case, slowly extracted a card, and handed it to Tom. "We're gonna need this right away."

Tom nodded and looked at the card. "You'll have it this afternoon, Lieutenant ..." he looked at the card, "... Biggs."

"I need it right away."

"I go off duty in two hours," Tom said.

"Not good enough."

"Best I can do," Tom said.

"You want me to talk to your chief?"

Standing where I was I could see that the back of Tom's neck had turned quite red.

"You know," Tom said, "what we have here is not exactly a hot pursuit. What we also have is some sawed-off state cop with a Napoleon complex. But here's the way it works, you file the right paperwork, you'll get my report. You don't, forget about it."

The lieutenant didn't back off. "Do you know who you're talking to?"

"Every cop in the state knows who you are and everyone I ever talked to has the same opinion. You're a guy who hasn't solved a case in ten years. You're in over your head and what you need to do is retire and get out of the way of the younger men who've got the training and the education."

"You know what you just did? You just wrote yourself a ticket to get fired."

Tom looked down at him and shook his head and grinned. "I guess you don't know our Chief. He used to work for you."

QUARRY

"It doesn't matter who he is. You think I can't go over his head?"

Tom shrugged. "I'll be sure to tell Brent that."

The guy cracked. Not much, but just enough to let us know that he knew who Brent was and it did not make him happy. But he couldn't back down. It was way too late for that.

"Just get me that report."

"You'll get it," Tom said, "when I get a request in writing."

The lieutenant suddenly whirled toward Jack and me. "Who are these boys and why are they here?"

"They called it in," Tom said.

The lieutenant looked at us, staring at me. "What were you doing here? Isn't this private property?"

"It's not posted," I said.

"We'll see about that."

Then Tom spoke up. "What? You're gonna charge these guys with trespassing?"

"Maybe they helped push the car into the quarry."

"Well, that about tears it," Tom said. "As of this moment you are in the middle of a crime scene and you have no authorization to be here. I'm ordering you to clear out and have the proper authorization delivered to the Chief before you set foot here again."

Mr. Hulm walked up. "We gonna haul the rest of them cars out today, Tom?"

The lieutenant looked around at him and stared.

"That'd be my plan," Tom said. "If you've got the time."

He laughed. "Unless someone rolls a semi, I got two other wreckers and crews. I'm the only guy who drives Big Ben," he said as he gestured with his head toward the wrecker.

"Good. Just have the rig ready. Upton says the bottom is smooth all the way so it should be quicker." He turned to the lieutenant. "You can leave now."

"I'll give you this, kid, you got a lotta sand. But maybe you're not too bright."

"Try me," Tom said.

The lieutenant turned away with his driver and walked back to their car.

Mr. Hulm laughed. "'Bout time somebody told that fool off. I've run into him too many times."

Tom grinned. "Probably wasn't the smartest thing I ever did."

"I didn't know a local cop could throw a state guy out of a crime scene," Mr. Hulm said.

"Nobody ever does, but there's a rule and I can make him follow it. Now he has to do the paper work."

"How's Brent figure into this?"

"He solved all of the guy's cases up until he took the job here ten years ago."

"World gets smaller every day," Mr. Hulm said.

Then the divers walked over to us, all four of them grinning and laughing. "That just made my day," Mr. Upton said. "You need somebody to back you up, you got four guys right here."

"Not worried about your jobs?" Tom said.

"They can't find good divers," one of the other divers said.

Tom looked out at the quarry. "What, exactly, have we got down there?"

"Some of those cars have been there a long, long time, Tom. They go all the way back to the thirties," Mr. Upton said. "And they're in surprisingly good shape. There's a forty-eight Mercury

QUARRY

flathead coupe I'd like to get my hands on." He smiled. "There's also a twelve cylinder Caddy."

One by one they towed the cars up onto land and it was like a scene from some horror movie. Each car had a skeleton in it and neither Jack nor I had ever seen such a thing even in a movie. Probably it was simply morbid fascination, but we looked carefully at every one and I was pretty sure I wouldn't sleep much that night.

We stayed until the last car came up and by then the forensic team had returned, this time with a box truck and a good supply of body bags.

While they worked, Tom talked on his cell phone. He was at it for some time and when he came back he was smiling.

"Can you guys run a computer?" he asked.

"Sure," I said.

"I've got a laptop in the cruiser. How about I get you logged on and then you can write out your statements and have that part of it over with."

So Jack and I went to work, sitting in the cruiser, typing out separate statements and filing them. It took a while, of course, and by the time we finished, all the cars had been emptied and the divers were starting to pack up.

"Is that all of them?" I asked.

Mr. Upton shrugged. "We still have to dive the other end but the water there runs well over a hundred feet. We'll need decompression gear and special air mixtures for our tanks. Don't hold your breath, though."

"You might not come back?" I asked.

"Nobody's gonna see this as urgent."

"What's your guess, Rich?" Tom asked. "More?"

Mr. Upton shook his head and pointed to the steep cliffs at the end of the quarry. "Only if there's a road up to there."

Mr. Hulm walked over. "Where you want these cars?"

"The state impound for now," Tom said.

"I take it you ain't been fired."

"The lieutenant's been taken off the case."

"Who's the new guy?"

"Gabriel Grange."

"Don't know him," Mr. Hulm said.

"He's the best they've got."

"What that means," Mr. Upton said, "is that somebody upstairs got the word and they're taking this seriously. Biggs would have buried the whole thing in paperwork."

"Why would he have done that?" Tom asked.

"It's what he does so he doesn't have to do any work."

Tom turned to us. "I want to thank you guys. You'll get a letter from the Chief, too, I expect."

"Can we call and find out what's going on?" I asked.

"Sure."

"Thanks."

"And you can do me a favor too. We've got a drug problem and suddenly it's getting bigger. I'd appreciate any help I can get."

"All I hear are rumors," I said.

"Anything is a help."

I nodded. I wanted to help, but it wasn't something I knew about and I wanted nothing to do with anyone who did.

Jack and I started walking back through the woods and

QUARRY

down to the stream where we had left the car, but a short way in I spotted an overgrown path headed through the woods to the right and I turned onto it. The trees here were maples and oaks, most of them tall and thick through the trunk so we knew they had been there a long time.

"Where are we going?" Jack asked.

"I wanna see where this path goes."

About fifty yards farther on we came to a building some twenty by forty feet. The weather had nearly worn away the letters on the sign by the door. It read: "Office".

And with the building came another mystery. Any old building like this, abandoned and with no one checking on it, got broken into. Not this one. The windows were covered with layers of grime but they were still there, unbroken, not even a crack in any pane. That the building showed no sign of decay, I assigned to its metal roof.

"This is so cool," Jack said as we rubbed away the dirt and tried to see in through one of the front windows. "We need to find out what's inside."

"Yeah, well not now with cops still here. Let's save this for another day."

He looked around at me, the safety guy, who never tried anything risky and from the way his eyebrows arched upward, I knew I'd surprised him.

"You'd do that?" he asked. "Just break in?"

"I wanna find out more about this place."

"You really are gonna break in?"

"Didn't see that coming, did you?"

"I should have," he said. "You never do anything the normal way. You don't even play lacrosse that way."

There was no path from the building to the stream so we cut off through the woods, climbed into the car, and put on our seat belts, both of us suffering from a mighty case of awe over what we had just seen.

"Would you really do that?" Jack asked.

"Do what?"

"Rat out a drug dealer."

"You mean am I afraid to rat 'em out?"

"What are you thinking here? Look, Cam, all those dead guys back there? How many of them were dead because of having something to do with drugs?"

I shook my head. "It doesn't matter," I said.

"What're you, on some kind of crusade?"

"You remember last year?"

"Jimmy Rawson."

"Who died from an overdose."

He shook his head. "I don't know, man."

"I do."

"He was an idiot, you know,"

"It doesn't matter."

"Yeah, I can see that." He grinned. "Guess I'll have to keep my ears open."

"All right." I started the car and we started talking about what we'd seen and then neither of us could stop talking. We babbled like a couple of excited girls all the way back to Jack's and then I headed home to tell my family about it.

I only live four miles from Jack's and I was about halfway home when I began to wonder whether the police would tell the news people who had reported seeing the car. If they did, would somebody come looking for us? No. It didn't make any sense. The cops would want to keep the guys who did it guessing. On the other hand, guys who killed people didn't seem to me like very rational types.

But what did I know about murderers? All I had to go on were novels and movies and TV shows, and all of it was fiction, even if all the stuff I'd seen and read was absolutely believable. Except for the stuff about firearms. They never, ever get that stuff right. Nobody counts the rounds and movie after movie, guns that hold six rounds are suddenly capable of getting off a dozen or more shots without reloading.

What I also knew was that sometimes you see things you don't know you've seen, and if someone else has a reason to think you might have seen something that could connect them to a crime, they might decide to whack you. That thought took some of the fun out of having such a fantastic story to tell. But I figured that would disappear pretty quickly once I started talking. It was, after all, a wild tale.

4... FISHING THE RIVER

On Sunday, Dad, Lance, and I got up in the dark, drove down to the marina, climbed into the boat, and headed downriver to several spots where we'd caught pike in the past. The fish we'd caught were small for pike, running five to six pounds, but at least we knew it was a spot the fish favored and that's always a good place to start.

The boat is a Pacific 26 with two Yamaha one-fifties and it flies. We were running with our lights on even though the eastern sky had begun to grow pale ahead of the rising sun. There was no traffic on the river and Lance drove the boat because Lance likes to drive the boat almost as much as he likes to fish. I think that'll change once he gets his driver's license, but that's about a year and a half away. In the meantime, he plays football and baseball and concentrates on growing. He's already six feet tall.

If he weren't my kid brother, I'd probably be jealous. I mean, what guy doesn't want to be taller? But I knew when I was twelve that nobody was ever gonna start calling me Stretch, so I went for tough. I ran and began lifting weights and playing lacrosse. Now

QUARRY

at five-ten and two-fifteen, I'm the big dog on the lacrosse field and just about anywhere else. It took five years to get there.

The air was cool as it usually is in April and we wore our rain-suits as windbreakers. The boat is open with only a center console so there's nowhere to get out of the wind, a consideration in a boat going forty miles an hour. I wrapped my arms around my chest to hold my rain jacket tighter.

The morning before, we'd taken several shad in the eight-pound class, and thrown back ten smaller fish, even though the shad were in a low population cycle.

No one seemed to know why, but most likely either they weren't finding enough to feed on at sea or something was eating the small shad before they got to sea and the striped bass seemed a likely candidate. The proof of that was the enormous number of stripers we'd caught using lures that imitate shad.

Some while ago, before I knew much about such things, the stripers had gone into decline. Then someone discovered that those fish don't spawn until they reach thirty inches in length and the legal limit was only sixteen inches. So they raised the limit to thirty-eight inches and the bass came back fast. Now the limit is twenty-eight inches and there are plenty of fish around, both schoolies and lunkers.

Today we were after fish that can run almost as big: northern pike. But those fish fight with a particular vengeance, slashing and leaping and thrashing and using their huge array of sharp teeth to try to cut through the line. It's why we use wire leaders.

Dad sat next to Lance on the bench seat at the center console and I rode on the seat in front of the console, watching the river, my eyes watering in the wind. In the rising light I stared at the water ahead, looking for any sign of fish. We were after pike but if a school of stripers surfaced, then we'd go after stripers. We are predators and predators never pass up a target of opportunity and that's absolutely true when it comes to fish moving in schools because they're there and then they're gone. The pike would be there because they occupy feeding territories

The fish that live in salt water and spawn in fresh water are called anadromous fish and there at least four major species in the Connecticut River: the stripers, the shad, Atlantic salmon and sea-run trout, though the latter two are rare.

I wasn't thinking about any of that. Instead my mind had locked onto the body and skeletons I'd seen in the cars pulled from the quarry. I wondered how many people had ever seen a dead body or a skeleton and I thought the number might be pretty small, especially when it came to skeletons, because most of those are six feet under the ground.

The images simply would not go away. They had turned up in my dreams but only as still images, which by the way, was enough to wake me up several times during the night. With that haunting me and my eyes a little weary from the lack of sleep, I almost missed the disturbance in the surface of the river. I only saw it out of the corner of my eye as we went past and then I signaled and Lance cut the engines.

What I'd seen showed in the wind-scuffed surface of the water as a smooth spot. Where there should have been ripples, the water had a glassy sheen. Somewhere upstream of that slick, fish were feeding, chopping through the bait, and the oil from the bait fish had risen to the surface and smoothed the water. There's an old saying about pouring oil on troubled waters and here was the proof that it happens.

The depth finder showed twenty feet of water and Lance

QUARRY

idled the engines and then moved the boat slowly toward the eastern shore. The depth finder didn't change, but as we drew closer the size of the area became clearer and we knew we were just downstream of a huge school of fish.

It was also a pretty good bet that they were in the twenty-inch range, school fish, most likely stripers. The pike rods were already rigged, so all we did was change lures to either Deadeye Dicks or Kastmasters, and Lance and I got ready to cast as Dad eased the boat past the slick, keeping off to the side.

Both of us fired our lures out ahead of the school and then reeled back fast with the current. It's a great way to fish moving water because it gives the fish only a short look at the lure.

"Whoa!" Lance shouted and hooked up and then I hooked up and Dad just held the boat in the current while we played the fish. Both stripers. Both about twenty-four inches long and that left them four inches below the legal limit.

We released the fish and I took the wheel, handed the rod to Dad, then ran the boat up behind the school again with the same result. At that point we knew we could go on catching those fish until the school disappeared and we decided to go after the pike. I made one last cast and this time I let the lure fall through the school because sometimes there will be bigger fish lying in the deeper water, picking off the scraps left from the schoolies feeding above.

This time I jigged the lure, pulling it up and then letting it fall, and about the third time I got a hit and it was a major league attack. My rod arced hard toward the water and I had to give line as the fish swept downstream of us, using the current to its advantage.

"Striper?" Dad asked.

35

"It feels tougher than that."

He had the wheel and we followed the fish downriver, but giving way very slowly so I could keep steady pressure on the fish. Bit by bit I gained ground and then it turned and ran and all I could do was give line or end up breaking off and I wanted to see that fish.

"Don't horse him," Lance said.

"Hey, little brother, I guess I know how to fight a fish!"

And then the battle changed. The fish was coming up and coming up fast and I had to reel as quickly as I could to keep the line taut. The fish smashed through the surface and I thought he'd never stop coming out of the water.

"It's a salmon!" Lance shouted. "You hooked a salmon!"

I'd caught landlocked salmon in Maine but this was an Atlantic salmon, the ultimate East Coast salmon, and he was huge. He dropped out of his leap and I felt him increase the beats in his tail and he came crashing out of the water, shooting nearly three feet into the air, shaking his head and trying to throw the lure.

QUARRY

You can't keep salmon because they're trying to bring back the salmon run in the Connecticut and now I had to concentrate on not damaging the fish which meant taking a very long time to tire him slowly so we could get him into the net, get the lure out of his jaw, and let him go.

Nobody had to say a word. We all knew that this would cut into the prime time for pike fishing but we had no other choice.

It took us an hour to get the fish next to the boat and Lance slipped the net behind him and we hoisted him up. Dad took a picture of me holding the fish with the blunt, rubber tipped scale hook in his mouth before Lance slipped the lure out of his jaw and lowered the salmon into the water, holding it in place to make sure it recovered. It took only seconds before the fish shot off into the deep water. Thirty-six pounds is what our scale had read.

My hands were shaking and I felt like I'd been lifting weights for an hour without a break.

I dropped onto the seat in the stern of the boat and just smiled. In fact, I couldn't stop smiling,

I think Dad and Lance were more excited than I was but celebration would have to wait.

"All right," Dad said, "we've still got time to try for some pike."

I jumped up. "I'll run the boat, you guys fish."

I got behind the wheel, took a deep breath, checked the engines, and then opened them up heading downriver to our secret pike hole, wondering what that salmon had been doing hanging around with all those stripers. Probably just a fluke, I thought, and then smiled to myself. No. That was another kind of fish and probably the best eating fish you can catch in the Northeast.

Fifteen minutes later I cut the throttles and eased the boat into position about thirty feet out from the bank of the river and then held it with the bow into the current as Dad and Lance began to cast toward the bank.

Sometimes we cast, sometimes we troll, though to tell you the truth there seems to be neither rhyme nor reason for the decision. One thing has always been clear. If you catch them trolling you won't catch them casting and vice versa. What remains is to figure out why that happens, though until we catch a pike that's willing to talk we'll probably never know and pike are not real talkative.

We made several passes casting and then dropped below the hole, let out line and trolled upriver about fifty feet from shore. When that didn't work we made another pass, closer to the bank.

"Let's try going with the current," Dad said.

To do that, we start upstream of the area we want to fish and then cut out into deeper water to let the lures sink and then cut back and make them rise. If fish are gonna hit, they'll hit the rising bait, and on the second pass, Lance's rod shot downward and out of the water came the biggest pike I'd ever seen. Man, what a nasty looking fish, with its long snout and those big sharp teeth. Their bodies are long and solid and they fight until they can hardly wiggle.

A lot of guys my age couldn't have handled it but Lance is one strong dude. He is also determined, a trait that kind of runs in the family. But he also knew he was tied into a fish that would hang on the wall in the trophy room and that had him pumped.

It took about forty minutes before Lance could lead the fish to the boat. Dad reached over the side and clamped onto the

QUARRY

fish's jaw, and then, using both hands, lifted it out of the water and into the boat. With pike, like bluefish, you have to be careful. More than one fisherman has wound up with some serious tooth marks.

Dad held the fish up and the scale read thirty-one and a half pounds. Using pliers, I took out the lure and Dad dropped the fish into the live well. And then we were jumping around, throwing high fives, and laughing. The state record was twenty-nine pounds.

"I think," Dad said, "we ought to call it a day!"

"You haven't caught a keeper yet, Dad," Lance said.

"I've caught plenty of 'em," Dad said. "But I want to get this pike up to Hank's Bait Shack and get an official weigh-in before he loses any weight. You've got a state record fish here and I wanna make sure you get credit for every ounce."

I ran the boat, to give Lance a chance to get quieted down, though I thought that might take about a week.

Just before we put into the marina I decided that as long as things were going so well, I'd spend the afternoon fishing for trout in the stream up near the quarry. I was sure Dad and Lance would go along.

Well, as it turned out they didn't go, but as it also turned out, Lance's pike weighed in on the official scale at thirty-three pounds and all that remained was to fill out the paperwork and file it with the state.

Was I jealous? Of course. Who wouldn't be? On the other hand, I was also pretty proud of my little brother who had fought that big fish perfectly and in the process given us all something to crow about. And then, too, there was the matter of the salmon. We had the weight and photo and I was pretty sure that while there was no official record for Atlantic salmon in Connecticut, that no one had turned up a bigger fish. It had also weighed more than Lance's pike.

Overall, we'd come out pretty even. The only real difference was that he'd get a giant fish to hang on the wall, but that was okay with me. Hey, he's my brother and younger brothers spend a lot of time thinking that older brothers have all the advantages.

And anyway, I'd have the picture on my wall.

Later, on the Internet, we discovered that the world record for northern pike is fifty-five pounds. It had been caught in Germany! I hadn't known they had pike in Europe.

Information like that always takes me by surprise. I mean, just when I think I know a lot, something turns up and blindsides me. It ... is ... awesome!

5... Working Upstream

The stream, a short way from the quarry, runs clear and cold but it's only about ten feet wide. Upstream of the bridge it runs down through thick groves of hemlocks, making casting difficult. The water runs fast and the fish are spooky, which is why most everyone fishes downstream where the land is more open and it's easier to cast. There, too, the water slows and the pools are deep.

But it only looks easier.

The banks are undercut and that's where the fish lie and it takes a perfect cast and drift to lure them out. You have to travel with a light foot, because your steps send vibrations through the ground and into the water and the fish go on full alert and won't take anything. Most fishermen get skunked whether they fish either upstream or down, which is, of course, why it's my favorite stream.

Usually, I fish downstream because the casting is easier, but this time I went upstream using my seven-foot trout rod with a four-weight line. The rod is an Orvis with a very fast action and because I was drifting nymphs it was the perfect choice, allowing me to set the hook the instant a trout picked up the fly. But it still took all the concentration I could muster. The nymph stays under water, out of sight, and when it drifts past a hungry trout, the fish slowly glides up and sips it into his mouth. That causes the line to stop for a millisecond and that's when you set the hook.

If your rod has a soft or even a medium action it slows your reaction time and that's important because the instant the trout knows it hasn't picked up a real nymph it flushes water backward through it's gills and blows the fly clear. The stiffer the rod, the more likely you are to hook a fish.

The neat thing about fishing a stream is that it's a lot like hunting. You know where the fish are most likely to lie and if you're careful, if you drop your fly in just the right spot and let it drift past the fish, they will rise.

And then some days nothing can tempt them. It was clearly one of those days because I'd gone nearly a mile upstream without turning a single fish.

I pushed on, and a short while later moved up into waters I had never fished before. My luck was no better and finally, I quit. My rod is a four-piece and I took it down and slipped it into the short tube and then zipped it into my light backpack.

Because I'd never been up here before, I decided to explore farther upstream. I walked slowly along the barely visible path, checking the pools, watching for any activity and wondering why I didn't even see any sticklebacks.

After a few hundred yards I came to a broad and well-used path that led off to the west toward the quarry. It looked to me like it had seen a lot of four-wheeler traffic.

Beyond where the path came in, the old trail was pretty well overgrown as if no one had walked there in a long time. I took that

QUARRY

trail and within fifty feet, I began to see dace and sticklebacks and now and again I saw a trout rise. I took out my rod and within minutes I'd hooked into a nice fat rainbow. I let him go and in the next pool up, I hooked a sixteen-inch brown. Suddenly, the mystery was more interesting than the fishing. What explained the dead zone between here and the bridge?

It didn't seem as if there could be many possibilities, and the best one, I thought, would have something to do with a chemical of some kind seeping into the water. To test that I'd need samples and to do that right I'd have to get sampling jars that were absolutely clean.

I took down my rod, walked back to where the new trail joined the old one, and began looking for any sign of seepage. I found nothing, though that only meant I couldn't see anything suspicious. If it came in along the bottom of the stream, and mixed quickly with the water, I would not have seen it and only by collecting a lot of samples could it be found.

I decided to see where the new path went. It's hard to measure distance on a trail that twists and turns, and especially when it begins to rise. I don't know why that is, but I suspect it has something to do with the amount of energy you use to climb, making the trail seem longer.

Anyone who plays lacrosse is in excellent shape. It is, after all, a game where you run all the time. But it's not just about the legs. You need time in the weight room in order to handle the stick and to ward off other players. Total conditioning is what I'm talking about here.

The trail turned north after a while and I stayed on it, looking back now and then so I'd know what things looked like when I headed back to the stream. Dad's woods training had started when I could walk. In new woods, you always looked back and established landmarks. These days that serves as a backup to a GPS, and I always carry that.

I reached the top of the ridge before I decided to save the rest of my hike for another day, because by then I was pretty sure this was just a trail made by kids with four-wheelers. It would be quicker, I thought, just to circle the quarry and walk back over the road to the car.

The barking dogs changed my plan. They sounded big and they sounded like guard dogs, and while I was not about to tangle with those dogs, I wanted to know what they were guarding.

I found a big old hemlock on what looked like a high point and climbed up to see if I could make out what lay ahead. I had the wind, so I guessed the dogs didn't know I was there, but I hadn't been all that careful when I'd been walking so they might have heard me.

I climbed a long way up that tree before I could see over the forest canopy and then I climbed higher and just as I reached the point where I could go no higher because the branches were too small to support me, I looked off to the northeast and I could see a large log cabin, a big barn, two four-wheelers, and two new pickups. The land had been cleared for some distance and there was a pasture with several horses and a few cows. There were also three dogs, contained in a high wire fence that surrounded the barn and I was pretty sure they were Rottweilers.

As I watched, two boys, probably around twelve, came out and fired up the four-wheelers. They headed off to a track they had made off to the east of the house and began racing. Man, did that look like fun! And those guys were good, making leaps and spins, all kinds of stuff.

QUARRY

In that part of town there is still a lot of country and from my perch I couldn't see another house. Off in the distance I could see a church steeple, which I thought must be in Hebron. I shrugged and climbed back down, thinking that once I got home I'd pull out the maps and see if I could locate the cabin and which road they took to get there. I always like to know what's around me. It cuts down on nasty surprises.

I also knew I wasn't going near that place. Anyone who chooses to live that far from people and surrounds the barn with a fence and free-roaming Rottweilers is not seeking company. But I could still find out who they were at the post office or even at the police station. Heck, I could ask Tom. He might even get a little curious himself. Maybe there was a reason why they didn't want company beyond simply being anti-social.

I swiveled around, looked the other way, and spotted the upper lip of the quarry, due south and maybe a quarter of a mile away at most.

Slowly, I worked my way back down the tree, picked up my pack and dug out my compass.

The trail I had been walking clearly led to the house, but as I thought about that, I decided that it came in pretty low on the mystery scale. Clearly, the kids had made the new path and that it went to the stream probably only meant that it went to the stream. So, no big deal.

I hiked to the quarry, using my compass and sighting ahead as far as I could see so I held a pretty straight line. I was on high ground and though it rose and fell there were no swamps I had to detour around and I came out on the edge of the quarry, across from where Jack and I had spotted the cars.

I'm always surprised at how different a place can look when

you change perspective, and the quarry was no exception. I walked to the edge and looked down at the water, but the sun angle produced only a reflection from this side, so I walked back from the edge and then swung to the north to circle the quarry, planning to walk past where we had first seen the car and then down to the landing.

The ground was strewn with huge boulders and it forced me to cut back into the woods and I hadn't gone far before I came to a low open rise. There were no trees, only grass and some low shrubs. I spotted an upright stone and then another and another.

It looked like a graveyard, but a very old graveyard. None of the stones had any markings and they had not been worked into any particular shape. They were just ordinary slabs buried deep enough to allow them to stand upright.

I took out my GPS, punched in the location, and saved it so I could find it again with little difficulty. Some might think that it would have been easy enough with the quarry so close, but unless you spend a lot of time in the woods, you're never quite certain where things can be found a second time without a lot of walking, and this mounded area was perhaps only fifty feet square. It probably wouldn't even show on most aerial photos.

Well, it would on the new stuff, the satellite stuff, but it would have to be very high resolution and most such sites on the Internet don't do that.

I turned back toward the quarry, looking for other places where a car could have been driven to the edge, but the ground here was broken and cracked into a lot of shallow, rocky ravines and I found no sign of anything having been disturbed for a very long time.

QUARRY

I walked the rest of the way to the landing and I had just started across it, headed for the road, when I stopped and looked off toward where the building sat, hidden by the trees.

I shrugged and turned toward the building, wondering if the police had checked it. But what reason would they have had? Nothing had happened there. I wondered whether they even knew about it.

I cut through the woods and walked straight to the building and this time I walked around it, trying to see through the dirty windows. When I reached the back, I did what we hadn't done before. I tried the handle. It turned. I pushed against the door and it started to open so I pushed harder and with the hinges wailing and squealing, the door swung back far enough to let me squeeze past.

It looked like a movie set for a building in a ghost town. The cobwebs hung in great drapes from the ceiling and even covered some parts of the walls. It was really cool. How long, I wondered, had it been since anyone had been in here?

A single big desk with a large faded green blotter and a leather chair sat near the back wall and several wooden chairs had been placed in front of the desk. There were black and white photographs on the walls showing the quarry in full operation, a coat rack, and then a door that opened into a small lavatory and another that led to the outer office. Both stood open.

I began scanning for a calendar. Every office had a calendar, but not this one. I walked out into the front room, taking things in, bit by bit, and when I turned I saw, in faded letters, the name on the door to the back office. It read: James Batterston, President.

It was what it looked like: the main office for a small quarry operation. But here's the strange thing. There were papers on the desks, pencils lying nearby. One of the file cabinet drawers was half-open and a file folder lay open on the files in the drawer. There were coffee cups in saucers on three of the four desks.

I felt like I was on sensory overload, trying to take in an enormous volume of information and sorting it into categories which later might fit into something recognizable.

I looked at the paperwork on the desks. One set showed the latest sales, and it was dated December 26, 1936. The day after Christmas. Another set of papers showed the sales for the year. I flipped the top piece over and it showed the sales for the previous year, about twice what the sales were for 1936.

About then my knowledge of history kicked in. It had been the height of the Great Depression. Businesses were failing and there were no jobs and there were bread and soup lines in the cities and people were fighting just to survive. It looked as if it had been no different here.

But who would have been buying granite then? Building was at a standstill, especially the kind of building that used the product this company produced. It was like seeing history first hand, and I could almost sense the desperation they must have felt.

James Batterston would have been laying people off, closing down operations, trying to hold together what he had left. And from what I knew about small businesses, from what I had heard about the Depression from my grandparents, most of the people who worked here would never have worked anywhere else. This was all they would have known and suddenly there was no place to work. How had they fed their families, paid their bills, bought clothes, and what had they done when one of their kids got sick?

QUARRY

At home we have a huge library and a great part of it is history. Dad studied history in college and he has always preached history to us as one of the most important things we learn. Mostly, he talks about economic history and how important it is to him in running his hedge fund. I thought then, standing in that office, that I was beginning to understand.

I walked into the back office, crossed to Mr. Batterston's desk, sat down in the leather chair, and looked out toward the front office, wondering what I could find out about him. Was there anyone left now who had known him? It was over seventy-three years ago. Someone twenty years old then would now be ninety-three!

Maybe the Historical Society had some records. Maybe stories had been passed down to the next generation. May... I stopped and stared at the floor and the single brass cartridge case which lay there. I stood, picked up the empty case and turned it over. It was a thirty-two auto.

I got down onto my hands and knees and I spotted the gun almost immediately back under the set of cabinets that stood behind the desk against the wall: a Colt like several Dad had in his collection, a small semi-auto, blued, but covered with a fine patina of rust. I fished it from under the cabinet, dropped the clip, and then jacked the slide back and a round flew out, landed on the desk, and then rolled off onto the floor.

I bent over to pick it up and that's when I noticed a big dark circle on the wooden floor. I got down onto my hands and knees and looked more closely. I was no expert but it sure looked like it could be blood. I stood up, reloaded the cartridge into the clip and slid the clip into the handle.

Someone had fired a single shot, dropped the gun, and it had slid back under the cabinet. Two possibilities came to mind. First that someone had broken in and shot Mr. Batterston and he had gotten off a round before he dropped the gun, or ... he had shot himself and the gun had flown out of his hand. The latter seemed more likely. But to be certain I sat back into the chair and aimed the pistol toward the door to the outer office. If Batterston had missed, maybe I could find a bullet hole in the wall, either here or out there.

I thought it was probably a wild goose chase but I marked an area on the far wall, walked into the front office, still carrying the pistol, and checked the area I had marked.

Nothing. But that still didn't eliminate the possibility, because a thirty-two is a pretty small bullet and there was a good chance that if it had hit someone it would not have gone through.

I walked back into the office, picked up the clip, and counted out the rounds. With one in the chamber the gun would have been fully loaded. And while hardly anyone does that now, the best way to keep your pistol ready is to keep a round in the chamber with the safety on.

Assuming he was here alone, then he might well have kept his pistol ready. I sat in the desk chair and scanned the room again, forcing myself to absorb each detail and that's when I noticed the winter overcoat and wide-brimmed hat hanging on the coat tree by the back door.

I checked the office again for another cartridge case and still came up empty-handed. I dropped the clip, the pistol, and the cartridge case into my pack and headed for the back door, noticing a large, old-fashioned key hanging from the lock on the inside of the door.

The key wouldn't turn so I opened my pack and took out the

QUARRY

little oiler I always carry there in case some piece of equipment might need a drop or two. I squirted it into the lock and then worked the key gently back and forth so I didn't break it off in the lock and slowly the mechanism began to move.

I stayed at it until I could lock and unlock the door from either side. While I was at it, I gave the door hinges an oil bath, then I stepped outside, locked the door, dropped the key into my pocket, and headed out to the road. It had been a day crammed with odd happenings, from the fish to the log cabin to the office, and when I added that to yesterday, I wondered if any two-day span in the rest of my life could match it.

I shook my head. Of course there would be such a time. In fact, probably hundreds of them. It was something no one could predict, which meant that thinking you had reached a high point in your life was most likely an illusion.

What was not an illusion was the test I had in American Literature at nine in the morning the next day and then later, lacrosse practice. We were a very young team with a new coach.

So far all the new coach had done was sit on the sidelines working crossword puzzles. The future did not look bright. Our best players had all graduated the year before and, aside from our goalie, I was the only senior.

We had gone from a state contender to a rebuilding year and we had a coach who had never played lacrosse. I felt like I was looking down a long dark tunnel.

6... THE KLUTZ

I want practice to be really nasty. That's the only way to get guys up to full speed, and just then I judged our speed at about the level of a hot tricycle. We'd already lost our first two games, not by a lot, but they were losses. Our coach said we were gaining experience.

What that amounts to is a big fat *So What!* You play to win. You win by beating your opponent. You beat an opponent by playing harder, working harder, and being smarter. You have to keep your head in the game, you have to take what the game gives you, and you never quit, even when you're behind or way ahead.

That is a list of what we were not doing. Everybody wanted to be a star and I didn't think there was much hope for change with a coach who had volunteered to take on the team because no one else was available. But then, nobody took lacrosse seriously. They treated us like guys who weren't skilled enough to play baseball or fast enough to run track. I figured it was time for us to wake up and smell the coffee.

But to do that we needed a coach who actually taught us something instead of sitting on the bench with his toucan-sized nose buried in a crossword puzzle. Maybe if we'd been just a bunch of wannabe jocks, I wouldn't have gotten so hot. But the facts were clear. We were good athletes who had played in club leagues every spring and summer and still did. And maybe with a good coach we'd be 2-0 instead of 0-2.

Like all sports, lacrosse requires a particular skill. You have to know how to handle the stick, how to catch and throw, how to use the stick defensively to prevent an opposing player from getting an open catch or throw, and how to bash another player without getting caught by the ref.

Gaining experience counts for nothing unless you under-stand what you have learned and then apply it. For that you need a coach. What we had was a cuddly little fat guy with a nose like Ratty in *The Wind in the Willows*, who taught English badly and did crossword puzzles, hoping to get into the national contest.

On Monday afternoon I began the takeover, the *coup d'etat*, the revolution. I called the guys together in the center of the field, had them form a circle around me, and I started. That I had any hope of bringing it off was a function of being a senior and having read half a dozen books on tactics and strategy. I had also played a lot more lacrosse than anyone else there, and every guy on the team knew that I was the nastiest player we had, and at times like that, nastiness counts. But it only has that effect if everyone understands why you're mad and that you're not mad at them.

"Okay, this is what's gonna happen," I said. "I'm taking over the team. I'm now a player and the coach. I say who plays. I say who sits. And I can guarantee this. Guys who don't work their butts off in practice will be sitting during games. Here is where we get it done. We'll begin with running. You're gonna run 'til you puke and then you're gonna run some more. If you don't like that, quit now."

I looked at them, turning slowly until I had looked into the eyes of each player. It was radical, it was off the walls, it was weird to have one of their teammates talking to them like a coach, but no one was fighting it. I'd heaved a challenge at them and they were gonna pick it up.

"When we finish running, we'll begin working on offensive strategy and tactics. We're gonna concentrate on position play and how to set screens and picks. Then we'll work the offense against the defense, shifting guys in and out until I find out which units are going to play together."

I clapped my hands once, hard. "All right. Windsprints. We start with windsprints."

I ran with them and I made it hard and then harder, making them sweat and groan and run. Amazingly, no one puked, and more to the point, no one quit.

Then came the instruction part, which was what I had been most worried about, but the stuff I'd read, the thousands of matches I'd watched, came together. And when they didn't do it right, I could step up and show them in slow motion and then full speed what I wanted.

For two hours we hammered away and I think I never spent a faster two hours. Best of all, it worked. They had come to practice as a bunch of individuals and now they were beginning to play together, to appreciate each other and to help the guys who didn't get it.

When I called it off a lot of tired, smiling guys left the field and Mr. Klutz called me over.

"Say, Cam," he said, "that was a pretty good practice."

QUARRY

I nodded.

"We'll have to do more of that, don't you think?"

I nodded.

"But we'll want to scribbage more, I think, maybe. Isn't that right?" He scratched his head. "Isn't that what you call it? Scribbage?"

"Scrimmage," I said.

"Oh, right, scrimmage. Got it confused with the card game. That's what we'll need to do, though, right?"

"When we're ready," I said. "Now it's fundamentals."

"Right. Absolutely. Fundamentals." He laughed. "Can't fly until you learn to walk, right?"

How, I wondered, could an English teacher do that? "I think it's 'you have to learn to walk before you can run.'"

"Sure. Absolutely right. Well, very productive, I think. We'll just keep it up. Next game is in only two days."

I nodded, turned away, and jogged up toward the gym and the locker room. I also made some changes there when I caught three guys leaving with dry hair.

"No way," I said. "This team showers after practice and games. You got a choice. Either get back in there and hit the showers or you're gonna be bench statues."

They were sophomores and all they could do was comply. Sophomores do not fight the big dog, particularly when the big dog is a senior and has just taken over as dictator.

I stepped into the locker room and I could feel the change in the air. It was electric. It was a room full of guys who were beginning to think they might win some games and they were excited and full of themselves. It's what you want. It's what you have to have if you're going to win.

At home, getting my homework out of the way before dinner, I thought about what I'd done. Where had it come from? What had caused me to suddenly start ordering people around? Tomorrow, I'd put it to them again and then the next day, just as hard, just as physical even though we had a game the following day. The schedule was in our favor because the next two teams were pretty weak and that would give us a chance to lay a foundation. Once you win you begin to believe you can win every time. It doesn't mean you will, it only improves your chances. The rest is done in practice.

After dinner, I got the pistol from the garage where I had left it until I had a chance to talk to Dad. He was in his office, a room off the back of the house crammed with all kinds of monitors and computers which he uses to keep track of the financial world. Hedge fund managers work all the time because markets are always open somewhere.

He also made a lot of money. I didn't know how much, exactly, but he did. I kept thinking that I'd get him to explain just how that whole thing worked, but I knew that too much of it would go right over my head. Maybe after I got through a couple of years of college and some economics courses, I'd be able to understand.

"What's up, Cam?" Dad asked as I walked up to his desk.

I took the pistol from my pocket along with the clip and set them on the desk.

He looked at the pistol sitting on his desk. "And thereby, I assume, hangs a tale."

So I told him the tale.

He picked up the pistol. "And this was just lying there on the floor?"

"It was under one of those credenza-type things."

"That is one heck of a story, Cam. You gonna pursue this?"

I nodded. "The library has a collection of old newspapers. I thought I'd go back to the ones around that date and see what I could find."

"Good place to start. Take notes. Take a lot of notes. There's a great story here, I think, and maybe you could write it."

"Me?"

"Sure. Why not?"

"I don't know. I guess I never thought of doing something like that."

"Just a thought." He turned the pistol over and over in his hands. "It was risky lugging this home, but it was smart not to leave it there."

"I was afraid some kid would get in there."

"Good thinking."

"I told you the back door wasn't locked, but the key was sticking out of the lock on the inside. I oiled the lock so I could turn it with the key and then locked it from the outside. The thing that's so amazing is that no one seems to have been in there in all that time."

"Probably just a function of who lives nearby, and, as I recall, the only houses are bunched down toward the brook."

"The stone houses," I said.

He nodded. "Must be a bit of history there. They were probably all built with stone from the quarry. The historical society folks might be able to tell you something about that." He reached out and tapped the pistol. "I'd just as soon you didn't mention this to anyone. If no logical heir turns up, we'll hang onto it. The rust is nothing. It'll come right off and, other than that, the gun is in almost new condition."

"What if it's a murder weapon?"

He grinned. "We'll wait until someone is charged."

"And if no one is?"

"You found it."

"Cool," I said, "that is really cool."

7... Worse to Weird

Okay, I'll admit it. I was feeling pretty chipper when I turned up at school the next morning. That lasted until I got a note to see the Athletic Director, Mr. Feuerbringer, directly after lunch. The guy's got the right name. In German it means fire bringer and he was nothing if not fiery.

But I wasn't worried. I figured he was going to congratulate me for getting the team on the right track. What can I say? I'm an optimistic guy. The glass, for me, is always half full and never half empty, the sun always comes back out, you get into trouble, you get out of trouble. I just never saw the point of moping around all the time like some gloom ball bent on making everyone around me miserable.

His door was open and I knocked on the jamb.

"You wanted to see me, sir?"

I was smiling, he was glowering, his brow pulled forward, his craggy face pinched to the middle. He looked like a thunderstorm looming on the horizon. Not a good sign.

"Yeah. Come in," he said, keeping his voice low and making it rumble like thunder in the small room, his eyes glinting like miniature lightning flashes. Really, really not good. In fact, kind of ugly.

I stood in front of his desk and he did not ask me to sit. I understood. In an office, the guy who sits is the one in charge. The guy who's standing is about to get his butt chewed.

"Correct me if I'm wrong, Bates, but the coach for your team is Mr. Klutz, isn't that right?" He tapped a piece of paper on his desk. "I know that because that's what it says on this paper here."

"Yes, sir. He's there every day."

"So that means he does the coaching, because he's the coach, or am I missing something here?"

I hate it when adults talk to you like you're stupid. Still, I kept my mouth shut.

"Because he's the coach, I'm wondering how it is that you decided to take over the team yesterday at practice."

"I didn't take it over. I just ran the practice."

"But you weren't told to do that by Mr. Klutz, were you?"

"He was busy with his crossword puzzle. I didn't want to interrupt him."

"And why would that be?"

"He gets kind of excited."

"That happens to coaches. It's part of the job."

I decided if he was gonna talk to me like I was a dummy, I'd give it back to him. "They get excited when people interrupt them when they're doing crossword puzzles?"

"That's not the point. The point is he's the coach and he tells you what to do. You can't be a coach because you aren't certified in CPR."

"I am certified. I got it last summer."

"But you don't have a coaching certificate, do you? Of course not!" He sat back in his chair smiling at me. "You gotta have that to be a coach."

"Yes, sir."

"So, from now on, Klutz runs practice, you got that?"

"Yes, sir."

"We have a chain of command here, Bates, and you have to go by that."

"Yes, sir."

He nodded. "You can go."

So I went. My ears were burning, the back of my neck felt like it was on fire, and all I wanted to was hit something ... hard! What really pissed me off was that I hadn't seen it coming. I had thought from my talk with Klutz that he was okay with my taking over practice. Of course, he hadn't actually said anything like that. He let me hear what I wanted to hear. Just a sneaky guy, a regular Iago, the guy in Shakespeare's *Othello*, who went around undercutting Othello. If you don't remember him then you probably remember Wormtongue in *The Lord of the Rings*.

Okay, at least now I understood.

I waited until everyone had changed into their practice gear and then I stood up, got their attention, and told them what had happened. Instead of one pissed off guy, I had twenty-eight pissed off guys, ready to tear the locker room to shreds.

It took me awhile, but I got them calmed down.

"Look, we can go on doing what we did yesterday. The difference is that I won't be calling the signals."

Jeremy Urbo raised his hand. He was a short kid, one of the sophomores and not much of an athlete, but he tried. It also turned out he was pretty quick at least when it came to thinking.

Don't let anyone kid you. It's a useful skill. "Would it be okay if we asked you questions? Instead of you telling us what to do next, we could ask, 'Hey, Cam, what's next?'"

It was what I'd been looking for. "Yeah," I said. "On the mark, Jeremy. But remember, I can only give you answers, not orders. From now on, you order yourselves around. You work together with your units and talk things over. Tonight I'll photocopy some strategy stuff for you but whether you memorize it or not is up to you." I opened a note pad. "I want all your e-mail addresses so I can send this stuff to you. It also gives us a way to stay in touch off the field. I want each of you to set up the team as a group on your e-mail, so you can send one message to the whole team at the same time."

They got it. A new game. Guys'll take every chance they can get to make an adult look stupid, especially if that someone is a teacher. It's a matter of payback for all the years of getting dumped on in grammar school and junior high.

We ran out to the field and Klutz was sitting there on the bench doing a puzzle and he never once looked up. The guys organized themselves into groups and ran windsprints and then took a break before starting on strategy and tactics.

At one point Kyle Rowan, a right-shooting wingman came up and asked me to help him with his stick work so I took him off to one side and demonstrated what I had been taught by my father who had been a really hard-nosed lacrosse player at Johns Hopkins, which year in and year out has one of the best college teams in the country.

Klutz came running down the sideline.

"Hey, Bates! Stop that. You're not to do any instructing. That's my job."

QUARRY

He stopped, gasping for breath after his mighty ten-yard run. I shrugged but he didn't see it because he was bent over at the waist. I thought he might even puke and I backed away as did Kyle. It was an ugly moment but it passed without incident.

"Now," he said, pulling himself up to his full five-five and turning to Kyle, "what was it you wanted to know?"

"My stick work is weak. I can catch all right but my throws don't have much on 'em."

I gave my stick to Klutz. "Maybe you can show him," I said.

He took the stick and gripped it with both hands as if he were about to begin.

"The basket goes at the top," I said.

He thrust the stick back at me. "This is not my role here. I'm focused on the bigger picture. I'm supposed to keep order and make sure things don't get violent. You show him."

"And that's okay?" I asked.

"Of course. I told you to. I'm the coach. As long as I tell you to do something like that, then it's okay."

I grinned to myself. He was never gonna get more than two words in any puzzle from then on.

I finished working with Kyle, then went from player to player telling them that whenever they wanted me to show them something, they had to ask Klutz first. Each time I ended with the same line. "You should probably ask him a lot of questions."

They got it and from that point on there was a line of players waiting to ask him permission to have me show them something. By the end of practice he was practically in tears and most of us could hardly play, we were laughing so hard.

Well, whattya think? Was I hauled into the Athletic

Director's office? Hey, does spring follow winter? Do cars ride on tires? Do girls like pink? He had his assistant, Mrs. Larabee, waiting for me at the door to the parking lot.

"What happened?" she asked. "I've never seen him so angry."

I shrugged. "We're having some difficulties with lacrosse."

"Not with your coach, I hope. Mr. Klutz is just the nicest man. Why, everyone simply loves him. Who wouldn't want to play for such a nice man?"

I let it go. I already had one revolution on my hands and fighting that one would be worse than the fight over keeping dodgeball in the gym program, which we lost. The administration was afraid someone might get hurt. Jeesh ... like the guy says, "you can't make an omelette without breaking a few eggs." It's also the kind of stuff that comes up when you get co-ed gym classes. What did they expect? All those girls, saying stuff to boys that if another boy said it, would have got him a fat nose, and we had no way to get back at them ... except in co-ed dodgeball. Man, it had been like shooting fish in a barrel, but even better because these fish squealed like stuck pigs.

I stepped into his office.

"Well, well, well, so here he is. The smart guy. You wanna explain what went on out there today?"

"Coach told me not to explain to Kyle how to improve his stickwork. But he said it would be okay to do that if Kyle came to him and then he told me to do it."

"That's all?"

"That's all I did."

"But Mr. Klutz was on the edge of a nervous breakdown yesterday. Something must've happened."

QUARRY

"The guys on the team had a lot of questions."

"What I don't understand is why he wouldn't show Kyle himself?"

"I'm not sure lacrosse was his main sport."

Now he looked at me, his eyes narrowed.

"I gave him my stick to show Kyle how to get power into his throws, but he didn't know which end was up. He told me his role was to keep order and prevent violence."

That's when he got it. "You can't take violence out of sports. You won't have sports!"

"Especially not lacrosse."

"Right. Absolutely right." He scratched his head. "This is what comes of not letting the A.D. make coaching appointments, and leaving it to the head hen. Okay, here's what I'm gonna do. I'm appointing you team captain. That gives you the authority to do what you were doing before."

I nodded.

"But don't think that makes you a coach."

"I don't have enough experience to be a coach," I said. "It takes years and years."

"You're darn right it does. Years and years and years. Good coaches are forged on the anvil of experience!"

I let that one go. Not only was it too easy but I had gotten what I wanted and it was time to shut up. But, man ..."the anvil of experience"? Where do coaches get that stuff? Maybe they have a guidebook of cliches for coaches.

8... BACK TO BATTERY

That afternoon, Klutz called us together in the locker room and announced that I was team captain and I would take care of all the instruction.

It was a true division of labor. I worked while he did crossword puzzles. I don't have anything against crossword puzzles. I do them all the time because it's a good way to develop the skills you need on the SAT's and for me that had paid off in the way they teach you how to recognize uncommon ways to use a word.

Consider the word run. If you say, "they run every day", run is a verb. If you say "they scored a run", it's a noun. So if the clue in the puzzle just says "run" you have to figure out which part of speech they want before you can get the answer. Go to the dictionary and look up "run". It takes more than a full page to cover all the possibilities. You don't have to read it. Just look at it. You'll get the idea.

Stuff like that is useful and I like stuff I can use. That's what practice is all about and that afternoon we had the best practice we'd ever had. Things began to come together. Guys began to make passes. They began to come up behind defenders, set picks to get a teammate loose for a run to the goal, and then roll off the pick to get open for a pass should the guy with the ball need help.

On defense, guys challenged, they went after the attacker's stick. In short, they had begun to understand the game. When that happens, practice doesn't even seem like practice. It's fun. Guys who have fun at practice, practice hard, and practices like that push you into winning games.

Even so, I wasn't counting on a win the next day. The only thing I thought we might do was keep their score down. We're strong on defense and maybe the best player on the team is our goalie, Barnaby Cadwallader. Okay, weird name but forget about it. Nobody calls him Barnaby. He's known as C-Shack. It started with Caddy then went to Caddy Shack and then to C-Shack.

He's quick as a striking snake and big enough to block a lot of the six foot by six foot goal with his body. In the other world, he's an outside linebacker who runs over the biggest people the other team has and spends his day sitting on opposing quarterbacks.

But perhaps the biggest surprise of the afternoon was that Mr. Feuerbringer showed up to watch. Every now and then adults take you by surprise. They change. When we had finished, he walked over and waited 'til I was alone.

"That was an outstanding practice," he said. "As good as any I've ever seen. Every player was working and learning. Now, this is confidential, but I'm gonna find you guys a real lacrosse coach. Until I do, Klutz will still be here because we have to have someone with a coaching certificate on the bench."

I grinned. "Thanks, Coach. We really need a guy who's played the game. You can only get so much out of books."

He slapped me on the shoulder and grinned. "Cam, what you've done here is very impressive. Let me ask you, where would you look for a coach?"

"One of the colleges, maybe a Trinity grad. They always have good teams."

He nodded. "Good coaches. They always have good coaches too. I'll give 'em a call, maybe there's a grad looking for work."

"That'd be awesome."

"Cam, I never watched lacrosse before and I had the idea it was kind of a ... well, not a real sport. Watching you guys this afternoon I got a different idea. You gotta have all the skills and ..." he grinned. "You gotta like contact."

"Who doesn't like that?" I said.

"Brings me back to the days when I played football. Every game was a war."

On the way home I stopped at the police station and asked for Tom. The patrolman at the desk smiled. "He's out back. He just finished his shift."

He made a call and a few minutes later Tom came out.

"Hey, Cam, how's it going?"

I nodded and smiled. "Well, things are going well."

He beckoned me to follow him and we walked back down the hall to a small office, went in, and he closed the door. "What can I do for you?"

"I wondered what you'd found out about the quarry."

He sat back in his chair and locked his big hands behind his head.

"So far the medical examiner says every one of them suffered a gunshot wound to the head. All executions."

QUARRY

"Wow ..."

"Later, he'll be able to tell us when they died and then we'll start searching missing persons files."

"You think you can catch the killers?"

He grinned and shook his head. "Our best hope is with the guy who was shot last week. He's been identified and it's pretty clear he was in with the Providence mafia. That means the FBI is gonna step in."

"I was hoping you'd get a chance to work on it."

"Me too. But that's the way it goes. It's out of my jurisdiction."

"But that won't stop you from looking into things here, will it?"

He looked over at me. "Is there a reason for me to do that?"

"Maybe everything hasn't been found."

"I'm guessing you found something."

"A couple of things. I fished the stream up from the road on Sunday and I found a four-wheeler path and followed it. There's a house and barn up there, way back in the woods. The barn is fenced-off and there are Rottweilers on patrol."

"Not very friendly sounding."

"Nope."

"How close did you get?"

"Not close. I climbed a big hemlock to get a look." I sat straighter in the chair. "Then I cut back over to the quarry and circled it to see if there was any other place where cars might have been pushed in but the ground there is all boulders and ravines. What I did find was an old graveyard."

He nodded. "How old?"

"I couldn't tell. At first I thought maybe it was an old Pequot burying ground but when I looked it up I found that they didn't use upright markers on graves." I shook my head. "I could be way off here, but I saved the coordinates on my GPS so you can find it if you want to take a look."

I took the GPS from my backpack, turned it on and called up the information I'd saved. Tom wrote it down.

"You are one nosey guy," he said and then laughed.

I grinned back at him. "I see things and then I want to know what I'm seeing."

"Seen anything at school?"

"Not yet."

"So what's this I hear about some guy catching a state record pike this weekend, some guy named Lance?"

"That'd be my brother. Thirty-three pounds."

"And then I heard that Lance's brother caught an even bigger Atlantic salmon. Any truth to that?"

"We had a good day."

"How was the trout fishing?"

"Weird. At first I couldn't even find any dace, then way up-stream I found dace and plenty of trout."

"Must've been the weather."

I shrugged. "More likely, it's just fishing."

"They're either taking or they're not."

"I'll probably try it again on Saturday."

"Lemme know how you make out."

It was the end of the conversation and I stood up. "Thanks for the information."

"What time's your game tomorrow?"

"Three-thirty."

"I'll try to make it."

QUARRY

"We're not very good yet."

"Doesn't matter."

I grinned. "No, it doesn't."

We don't eat until seven, which left me time to stop at the library and begin looking through old newspapers. Everything is on computer there now and I just picked out the year I wanted.

Before, I had only read the history of the Great Depression, but these stories were about the people who lived through it and I'd had no idea what they had gone through. I had to make myself focus on the information I wanted. I typed Buckingham Granite into the search box and hit the button.

It found ten stories and I read each one carefully. The short of it was that the Depression had killed the business. At the high point, over a hundred men had worked that quarry, cutting a very high grade of fine grained gray granite that had been used in buildings all over the country. When the company closed, they had only ten people left working for them.

But the stories only said that the company had closed. So I searched, using the name of the owner, James Batterston, and this time I set the search parameters for ten years either side of the closing. Things began to turn up. Mr. Batterston had served three terms as first selectman. He'd been a deacon in the church. He and his wife had raised two sons, both of whom went off to Yale where their father and grandfather had gone. The Batterstons had frequently hosted fund-raisers for their church and other organizations in town.

I found an article from 1933 about the older son graduating from Yale Law School and then another one in 1936 about the younger son graduating from Yale Medical School.

Finally, there was a death notice and a long story about James Batterston. He had died just over three weeks after he'd closed the doors on Buckingham Granite. It did not say how he died, but obituary notices seldom do. In that story it listed his wife, Elizabeth, and their sons, George and Harry, as survivors. George, the lawyer, lived in Boston, and Harry, the doctor, lived nearby in Farmington, or they had at the time. I wondered if they were even alive now.

Four years after the article had appeared we were fighting two socialist nations, Germany and Italy, and one monarchy, Japan. A lot of men died.

I removed the disk from the machine and took all the disks back to the desk.

"Find what you were looking for, Cam?" Mrs. Maloney asked as she took the disks I handed her.

"I don't think so."

"If you want to know more about the Batterstons you ought to get it from the source. Harry is still alive, retired now, and living here in town. He's quite old but you ought to go see him. He's very sharp and he likes having visitors. Mrs. Donne keeps house for him and she answers the phone. If you'd like, I'll tell her to expect your call."

"That would be great," I said. "Thanks."

"My pleasure, Cam."

The words sounded harmless enough, but there was a tone in her voice I didn't understand. It sounded as if she were eager to have me digging into the past. That made me think there was a good deal more to the story, and suspicion fires my curiosity.

I also wondered how she knew I had been looking up the Battersons. The disks had been for the local newspaper.

9... LACROSSE

I sat at my usual window table in the cafeteria, munching away on a roast beef grinder, when Jack set his tray on the table and sat down.

"I hear you're king of the lacrosse team now," he said, grinning in his usual ironic fashion.

"Absolutely. King, tsar, ruler, monarch, take your pick." I bit into my grinder.

"I thought a monarch was a butterfly. You a butterfly?"

"Only in one respect. I'm every bit as dogged."

"Okay, you lost me there."

"All the monarchs around here fly twenty-five-hundred miles back to Mexico to winter over and breed and then their offspring fly back here in the spring and breed."

"Whoa, wait a minute. How do the new ones know how to get here or even where to go?"

"It's one of the great mysteries."

He laughed. "Speaking of mysteries, did you find out any more about the bodies?"

"They were all murdered. Each of them has a bullet hole in

the skull."

"That is awesome! A mass murder in our town?"

"Not exactly. They were killed one at a time, not all at the same time."

"Let's not get too picky here."

"Stick to the facts, only the facts."

"Well, I found out something too. My grandfather once worked for the guy who owned Buckingham Granite."

That got my attention. "Really?"

He nodded. "He was a clerk in Batterston's office."

"How long was he there?"

"A couple of years."

"Try this on," I said and then told him what I had found in the office, which pretty much blew his doors off. "Would your grandfather talk to me?"

"Sure. He's pretty old but his memory is still perfect and he loves talking about old times."

"Cool."

"What do you think happened there?"

"In the office?"

"Yeah."

"If the stain on the floor is blood, somebody got shot."

"Whoa ... you think?"

"I can't come up with any other way to explain it," I said.

"Another murder there? What are the odds of that?"

"Pretty long, but not impossible."

"But not improbable either?" He took an enormous bite out of his ham and cheese grinder.

"Maybe your grandfather can tell us something about Batterston, like what kind of a man he was, whether he suffered from depression."

All he could do was chew.

"Maybe he committed suicide."

Jack swallowed. "Can we find out whether the stain on the floor is blood?"

"It happened a long time ago. There's a chemical they can use but I don't know whether it would work on something that old."

"What kind of chemical?"

"I think it's called luminol or something like that."

"So we get a jug of it, spread it on that stain, and see what happens."

I grinned. "I'm gonna guess you don't find stuff like that just lying around on a shelf in the drugstore."

"What about Mr. Canfield?"

"You think he keeps that in his chemical locker?"

"He's got a lot of weird stuff in there, Dude."

"What do we tell him we're gonna do with it?"

"Look for blood."

I laughed. "The truth shall make you free."

"That sounds familiar."

"It should. Jesus said it."

"Smart guy," Jack said.

"Yeah, you think?"

"Pretty smart thing to say."

I nodded. "If he were running for office."

"He was," Jack said.

He's always been one of those guys who is sneaky smart. "So" I asked, "what else do you know about Canfield?"

He grinned. "He's into forensics. He worships Henry Lee.

And he's got a kind of a ghoul thing going."

"Well, that's pretty cool."

"Tomorrow, after class?"

"Worth a try."

"You guys got a chance today?"

I shrugged. "We're still trying to find out if we can keep the wheels on. But we'll see. We could hold our own, I think. If we were playing somebody else, maybe not, but against New Milford, at least this year, we've got a chance."

"Then maybe I should go to the game."

"You're saying you only go if we can win?"

"Nobody wants to watch a loser, Dude."

"I thought you were my friend," I said and he knew I was needling him.

"That's got nothing to do with it."

"How many of your swim meets have I gone to?"

He grinned. "But we always win."

"You mean *you* always win."

"Hey, I'm an awesome swimmer."

"And not afraid to tell everyone."

He had been about to take another huge bite but then he set the grinder on its wrapper. "You never do that, do you?"

"Nope."

"Why not?"

"When we're winning I don't need to and when we're losing it means I have to work harder."

"That's why when you were winning last year you never said anything."

"We went all the way to the semis, right?"

He hoisted his grinder, took another big bite, and about then

QUARRY

a bunch of kids grabbed the seats at the other end of the table and that kind of killed the conversation. It was just as well. We both had a lot of eating ahead.

Lacrosse matches generally don't draw much of a crowd and the game against New Milford was no exception. Maybe twelve people showed up. I think anyone who's ever played a sport dreams of playing in front of a mob of screaming fans, but I was not disappointed. The younger guys have trouble focusing in front of crowds.

I suppose it sounds like boasting, but in fact, our game was built around the defense: Rick Reich, Bobby Green, and me. Rick and Bobby are juniors with two years of high school experience. Behind us is C-Shack, a senior and an All-State goalie.

You'll hear it over and over, no matter what sport you play, and it's true. Defense wins games. And against New Milford, our defense was clicking. We play man-to-man because we're fast enough to cover their fastest attackers, preventing them from getting open passes and we're strong enough so they can't knock us down (well, most of the time) or push us out of the play.

In the first period we never let them get a single shot on goal and while our offense is green and young they are quick and they can all shoot. The guy who looks like he's getting it together fastest is Ray Hammond and he scored our only goal, cutting off a screen, spinning past another defender, taking a high pass, spinning again, and firing a rocket past their goalie.

For anyone who hasn't played or seen lacrosse, it is a wide-open game with people running and moving constantly to get position. You can hear the clash of sticks a long way off as players hack and hammer away at each other.

During the first quarter break I sat the guys down and explained what they were doing wrong and how to improve. They listened, wiped the sweat from their faces, drank some Gatorade, and as I looked into their eyes, I wondered how much they'd really heard.

"It's a lot to take in all at once," I said.

Tyler Maine, our pointman, shook his head and looked up at me. "How come the defense doesn't get criticized?"

I pointed to the scoreboard. "You see where it says New Milford? You see the number under the name? Zero. We can't do any better than that."

The rest of the guys smiled and then Maine grinned kind of sheepishly. "Got it," he said.

"Okay. Remember this. Set more screens. When you come off a screen, come off as fast as you can run. If you're making a pass, lead your man so he can catch it at full speed, in stride. And remember this. Try not to get hit and try not to hit anyone. When that happens it throws off your rhythm and lowers your chances of making a clean shot."

The ref blew the whistle to start the second period and I pulled the team into a huddle so we could all put our hands together. "Victory!" I shouted and then we all shouted it.

The second period also belonged to our defense and theirs. They gave up one more goal and we gave up one. C-Shack was awesome! The only shot he didn't stop was a ricochet off the helmet of one of New Milford's attackers.

But we were still playing the game at the wrong end of the field because our offense was out of synch, and I think a little awed by the guys from New Milford. What we needed was someone on offense who could lead, who could score. By next year our

QUARRY

young players would be there but now, with not enough experience, with too few skills, it was up to the defense to carry us and by the fourth quarter we'd be sucking wind. We'd be a step slow and that's when they'd hammer us.

As we sat on the empty bleachers at halftime, I just let the guys cool out. I knew I was supposed to have some rouser of a talk to get them pumped up for the second half but I couldn't think of a thing to say.

I tried, but it was like running into a brick wall, it was like trying to think of something to say when I was face-to-face with a pretty girl. My brain, at least the talking part, was in neutral and I couldn't shift into drive.

Coach Feuerbringer rescued me.

He walked up and stood in front of us. "Listen up here a second," he said. "I liked what I saw out there in the first half. You played together. You played the way a team, any team, is supposed to play. Nobody hogged the ball, nobody tried to be the star. As Athletic Director, I'm proud to say that you guys play here. You're a credit to the school, to yourselves, and the game." He paused and let his words sink in. "I expect you to win. I expect you to go on winning and you will as long as you play the way you have so far. I don't want to see any letdown. I want to see you work harder. When they run fast, you run faster! When they play smart, you play smarter!" He clapped his hands together so hard it sounded like someone had fired a starter's gun. "Now go get 'em!"

I don't know whether that was the best halftime speech I ever heard, but it had just the effect we needed. Over the next two periods we slowly pulled away and by the time the final whistle sounded we were up six to two. That's kind of a low score for a lacrosse match, but it was gonna send a big time message to other coaches. We played defense and we had enough offense to get the goals we needed to win. Shows you what you can do if you push as hard as you can the whole time you're on the field.

Two days later we met our new coach, Hank Bradford. He'd played the goal for Trinity for three years and he was working on a master's degree in math.

Sometimes you look at someone and you just know. We knew. We also had some facts to go on. This guy had played the game and played it well. He had a huge reputation and because Trinity was only two towns away, most of us had seen him play. He also got off on the right foot.

"I saw your game against New Milford," he said, "and while there's room for improvement, you guys are gonna get there. For now we're gonna stay with man-to-man on defense and a one-two-two offense. We'll build from that. Your captain will still be Cam Bates."

That brought a cheer and I smiled and waved.

"Now, are you guys ready to practice?"

Man, we shot out of the locker room and ran full speed for the field. For the first time it felt like all the good stuff was in front of us.

No team wins without a good coach and now we had one and we were pumped.

I also had an idea about how to improve the offense ... fast.

10 ... MR. CANFIELD

Jack and I met with Mr. Canfield before practice. I don't think I'd ever really thought about how strange he was until we sat at the table in the lab and I watched his face light up when we described the bodies from the quarry. He looked like he'd start drooling at any second and I had the feeling that this was a guy who spent all his free time hanging around morgues and watching zombie movies.

The fact that he is tall and skinny with glassy eyes and thinning black hair that he combs over his bald spot reinforced the image.

When we finished talking, he sat there looking at us and then, suddenly, he began rubbing his hands together like someone about to sit down to a delicious meal. That's when I wondered if maybe I'd been watching too many zombie movies.

He cleared his throat and nodded his head and looked down at the table and when he looked back up, he seemed like the guy we usually saw in front of class.

"I do in fact have the chemicals you need, but I'd like to offer you a proposition. I want to be there. I'm a chemist and a pretty good chemist, even if I never went past my master's in chemistry. I've also spent years studying forensics. I took Henry Lee's courses, I've read everything I could find and this year I'll take the state exams. But I have never gotten to see a murder scene first hand and this seems as if it would be perfect."

Maybe if I hadn't been so eager to find out what had happened in that office, I wouldn't have agreed so quickly. But there was something in the way he talked now, his voice calm and rational, that made me think he could help us explain a lot we hadn't been trained to see.

"Once I've passed the exam and I have my license I'll be applying for jobs in forensics but my lack of experience will be a problem. This would give me the opportunity to document my abilities and do what I've wanted to do for a long time." Suddenly he swiveled his head, looking first one way and then another, as if he were afraid someone was watching. "Please, whatever you do, don't mention this to anyone. No one knows about this and I don't want them to know until I give my notice to the Superintendent."

It hadn't occurred to me to talk about it, but now I would be certain to keep my mouth shut. What was the saying from World War II? "Loose lips sink ships".

"We won't say anything."

"Good. Good."

"Do you think you can solve this?"

"Solving cases is up to detectives. My job is to say what happened and how it happened. That opens up leads and possible suspects."

I looked at Jack and he nodded. "Do you know how to get to

the quarry?"

He shook his head. "I live in Marlborough. All I know is how to get to the school."

I pulled a map from the front pocket of my backpack and handed it to him. "The only hard part is locating the road into the quarry. It's pretty much overgrown." I pointed to the map. "When you come around this bend the turn is on your left just before the road begins to straighten. If you come to the stone houses, you've gone too far. I'll leave an orange survey ribbon around a tree just before the road."

He nodded, folded the map, and put it in his pocket. "When do you want to meet?"

"Saturday at one. I'm fishing in the morning."

"Couldn't we do this after school?"

I shook my head and grinned. "Lacrosse practice."

"There won't be any trouble about going into the building, will there?"

"Nobody even knows it's there. The back door was unlocked and I don't think anyone's been in that office since it was closed in the thirties." And then another thought occurred to me. "The only guy I can think of who might turn up would be Tom Kiernan. He's a local cop and a really good guy."

"Can he be trusted?"

I nodded. "Yeah, he can."

"He's okay," Jack said.

"Does he know anything about investigations like this?" Mr. Canfield asked.

I grinned. "He was pretty much pissed that he had to turn the investigation of the bodies in the quarry over to the FBI. But this would be something separate from that. Maybe he'd even like to work on it."

"What do you know about the people connected with Buckingham Granite?"

"I'm still putting some stuff together. I've got two people to interview and I've got the stories from the newspapers back then. I hope to have it finished by the weekend."

"What exactly are we looking for?" he asked.

"I thought it might work better if I just left you to figure that out from whatever evidence you find."

He smiled, well I guess it was a smile, or maybe it only seemed like a smile.

"Hey," Jack said as we walked down the hall toward the locker room and the back door to the parking lot, "I'd like to go up there and look around. Would that be okay?"

"As long as you don't go into the office and don't touch anything. And be careful. There's some guy living in the woods about a mile away and his place is surrounded by chain link fence and there are Rottweilers inside the fence."

"Probably some guy growing marijuana."

"Or just a crazy of some kind." I stopped at the door to the locker room. "Maybe it's not a good idea. You might disturb something."

"What could be left after over seventy years?"

I shrugged. "Hey, I'm not a forensic specialist."

"I see your point."

"I thought you were working out in the pool today."

"I am."

"So it's not like you have nothing to do."

"Sometimes I get tired of swimming laps."

QUARRY

"You used to play lacrosse. What happened to that?"

He shrugged and looked down at the tiled floor and I knew what that look meant. His mother had made him quit. Some parents do things like that. She was probably afraid he'd get hurt. Jack had once been an excellent lacrosse player. He was tall and fast and he'd played the point on the attack. Still, that was five years ago, when we were just twelve and things change.

"We could use a guy at the point," I said.

"Yeah?"

"Absolutely." I laughed. "Different muscles though. You'd be hurting."

He was thinking about it.

"You used to be really good. Why not give it a try. We've got a new coach, a guy who knows the game." I dropped my hand on his shoulder. "Hey, you go to the games, you know what's going on out there. I'm not saying you'll step on the field and start, but you'll get some minutes."

He didn't want to say what was holding him back so I said it for him. "I promise not to tell your mother."

He laughed, his embarrassment clear. "She won't be a happy camper if she finds out."

"But she won't be going to any games. She'll think you're still swimming laps."

"But what if ..."

"Never mind that stuff. You're old enough to decide which sport you want to play."

That got to him. "Okay. I'll watch practice and maybe I'll talk to the coach. You guys were awesome yesterday. I liked the way you played together."

"If you're serious, let me know and I'll talk to Coach first. It'll be better if he knows something about you."

He nodded. "See you out there."

What a practice! It was totally physical from start to finish and Coach Bradford worked us hard and nobody minded. He wanted us to be ready, to have the stamina to play at full speed for an entire game if we had to. It also allowed him to identify the slackers.

When he worked with the offense, I ran the defense, when he worked with the defense I ran the offense, making them work on each set of skills until I thought they were gonna fall down from exhaustion.

But they didn't. They kept at it, we all kept at it until Coach blew the whistle and called it a day. I walked over to where Jack was sitting on the bleachers. "What'd you think?"

"This guy is nasty. But here's what I saw. I saw a bunch of guys working their butts off and nobody quit trying." He grinned at me. "But it'll be hard to adjust to having you tell me what to do."

"You'll get used to it. You want me to talk to him?"

"Yeah. I want to play."

"Awesome!"

I walked over to where Coach Bradford was standing, look-ing down at his notes.

"Coach?"

"Yeah, Cam?"

"There's a guy sitting down at the end of the bleachers, Jack Waverly. He used to play lacrosse when we were younger but then he went over to swimming. He was very good when we were younger and he's an All-State swimmer."

He glanced down toward Jack. "What events does he

QUARRY

swim?"

"Sprints."

"Good start," he said.

"Would you talk to him?"

"You sure he's up to this?"

I grinned. "I told him he'd have some pretty sore muscles for a while. But he is a very tough guy. He used to play the point." That got his attention because we were very thin at that position.

"Okay. After I say a few words here. I'll talk to him."

"Thanks."

I sat on the bleachers and gave Jack the thumbs-up.

"Okay, listen up here," Coach said, "you guys have the makings of a good solid team. You showed that today. We've got plenty to work on, but I liked what I saw out there. And I liked what I saw on the field yesterday. Normally, we wouldn't have a practice on Friday or on the weekend, but this isn't a normal situation. Next week we play one of the better teams in the state and we've got to be ready.

"So, same time tomorrow and one o'clock on Saturday." He waited for the groans but he heard none. He smiled. "See you then."

I waited for Jack and then we walked back up to the locker room.

"What'd he say?"

"He told me to get my gear and be here tomorrow." He shook his head. "Do you think he'll be this tough all the time?"

"I'm pretty sure you can count on it."

"I like tough coaches. Those kind of guys get you to where you can win."

I slapped him on the shoulder. "Come over tonight and I'll

get you equipped. I've got extras of everything. The only thing I don't know about is shoes."

"Got it covered. I'm headed to the store now." He slapped his hands together. "This is so cool. Even if I don't get into a single game it doesn't matter. I already know most of the guys on the team and they're guys I get along with."

"I think this is an excellent move," I said.

"Yeah. Me too."

"I'll tell Canfield we have to switch to Sunday," I said.

"What did you make of him?"

"Whattaya think?"

"Strange dude, huh?"

"Right on the edge of weird," I said.

"You having second thoughts?

I shook my head. "Nope. I have the idea that this could be very interesting."

He laughed. "Interesting is a dangerous word."

"It is," I said.

11... Information

Anyone else and I'd never have done it but Jack is absolutely jacked and he is in peak condition. He's strong as an ox and he can run and he has really quick feet and none of that had changed except that he was in a whole lot better shape than any of us had been five years ago.

The only downside was that, like most swimmers, his strength was mostly upper body. Lacrosse is a game where leg strength is vital because it's not just running, but cutting from side to side, stopping and starting, and I figured he'd play out pretty quickly.

I couldn't have been more wrong. His legs were in great shape and he'd forgotten none of the game. And when he played the point, stuff began to happen. His passes were like lasers, accurate and thrown where the wings could pick them off.

I spent my time working with the defense and Coach spent the whole practice with the offense because that's where we were in trouble.

For the last half hour we scrimmaged. The defense gave them nothing. They never got a shot on goal and then Coach put Jack in and everything changed. He was so strong that you couldn't body him out of the play, and because of his height and the width of his shoulders, when he was carrying the ball, it was almost impossible to get to his stick. And then there were the elbows, sharp and powered by those shoulders, you only got hit with one once and then you stayed away.

For the first time in a practice, C-shack got some work. He stopped every shot on goal until Jack made a pass, rolled off a screen, picked off the return pass on the give-and-go and fired a shot so hard I thought it would tear out the back of the net. C-Shack never had a chance. Jack's stick just twitched and the ball was past and into the net.

Suddenly, the guys on offense could hold up their heads. They even began to swagger. That's when Coach called the practice. He wanted them to go home with their chins up, their confidence high.

Jack and I walked to the locker room.

"Awesome shot, big guy," I said. "Looks like you remembered how to play."

He grinned. "I think all the swimming paid off. I didn't know I could get that much on it."

"How're the legs holding up?"

"They're fine."

"No knee wobbles?"

"This past winter in practice I started working on the three-meter board."

"You've been diving?"

"Yeah. I wanted another event. There's too much sitting around at meets. I swim three events, the hundred, two hundred and the 400 medley, but mostly I'm just sitting. It gets kind of

QUARRY

boring." He laughed. "This is perfect. There's no boring in lacrosse. There's only catching your breath when the play moves downfield."

"This is so cool!"

"You think?"

"Yeah, I think."

"Did you talk to Canfield?"

"We're on for Sunday."

"If you want, we could go over to my grandfather's tonight."

"That'd be awesome. Tomorrow I talk to Dr. Batterston."

"Who's he?"

"He's the son of the guy who owned the quarry."

"Wow. How'd you find him?"

"The librarian, Mrs. Best. She knows everyone in town."

"So you'll have a bunch of stuff for Canfield."

"A ton."

I had noticed his change in wardrobe earlier in the day. He was wearing jeans that fit and didn't sag. His shoelaces were tied and he had on a polo shirt. But not until we were walking out of the locker room did I say anything.

"Good change," I said.

"What?"

"Your clothes. Especially the jeans and shoelaces."

"I wondered if you'd noticed."

"Hard not to."

"Yeah, well, playing for a coach like Mr. Bradford ... I figured the homey look wouldn't do me any favors."

"Be my guess." I laughed. "On the other hand after that shot you made, he might've overlooked a lot of things."

"You think?"

"He may never have seen anyone get that much speed on a shot before. Did you see C-Shack's double take? I don't think he even saw the ball."

"Hey, I'm lovin' this. Go ahead. Build my ego. More! More!" He laughed. "Is this gonna be fun or what?"

Jack's grandfather is a tall man, bent slightly now with age, but he doesn't look anything like a man in his eighties. His blue eyes crackle with energy and there's nothing slow about his thinking or his memory.

We sat in his living room, and he had a fire going in the fireplace against the chill of the April evening.

"So you'd like to know about Buckingham Granite, which I assume means James Batterston. I was his office boy for two years after I got out of high school. After Jack said you'd like to know something about him and the company, I began thinking back to see how much I could remember. I think I surprised myself.

"What I remember most was that he was friendly and easy to work for, but he was also a stickler for detail. He expected everyone to work hard and do their job correctly. The wages were fair and I never heard anyone, either in the office or in the quarry, complain about being underpaid.

"He was the first to arrive in the morning and he locked the place up at night." He looked over at Jack. "Say," he said, "I'm forgetting my manners here. Jack, there's some Coke in the fridge, and if you wouldn't mind, could you get us some? Bottles are fine, unless you want glasses."

When Jack left the room, he turned and looked at me. "Jack tells me he's playing lacrosse again."

"He's much better now," I said, "and he was good then."

QUARRY

He smiled. "Until my daughter-in-law finds out."

I shrugged. "Guys gotta do what guys gotta do."

"No question there. I think I'll be going to the games, at least the home games. Don't drive at night anymore, eyes, you know, but all your games are in daylight. I never missed a home swim meet either."

"Neither have I."

He nodded. "You two have been friends a long time."

"Since first grade. We just kind of got along."

"It's a rare thing. Friends often grow apart as they grow older, or so it seems to me."

"Not us."

"Not likely that'll ever change now."

"I guess we'll have to see how it goes."

"With college, you mean."

I nodded. "New places, new friends."

"Never went 'til after the war. When the quarry closed I joined the Navy and went right on through 'til it was over. Ended up as a pilot and after the war I went to college and got my degree in engineering and then I went to work for Pratt and Whitney and stayed until I retired. I lost two of my high school friends in the war but there were others and when I came home we didn't seem to get along so well. Maybe it was because I'd been an officer and they were enlisted."

Jack came back and distributed the Cokes, big, sixteen ounce babies, frosty cold just the way I like them.

Mr. Waverly smiled. "I'm gonna do some talking, this'll keep my whistle wet." He took a swallow and set the bottle on a coaster on the small round table next to his chair.

"Let me get to the thing nobody would ever talk about. James

Batterston's so-called heart attack." He waved a hand through the air as if to dismiss the notion. "He was found in the office with a bullet through his head. The town was very small then and the family was enormously powerful, even more powerful than the tobacco families, so it was easy to hush things up. Officially, he died of a heart attack brought on by the stress of having to close the business his father had founded.

"But it was a bullet and not a bad heart that ended things for him and I know, because I found the body. It was the day after he'd closed the place and I'd left some things in my desk. When I went back, I found him on the floor of his office."

"It must have been awful," I said.

"Well, it was. No denying that." He drew a big, long-fingered hand over his mouth and chin. "Terrible thing. I went out to the front office and stood there looking at the phone, trying to decide whether to call the family or the police and finally, because I didn't want to be the one to tell the family, I called the police.

"Then I went back into the office and looked around because at that time I never thought about suicide and I think that was because I never thought of him as a man who would do that. He'd always been cheerful and positive and even the day before when he told us he was closing down, he said he hoped that if business picked up in the next few months, he would reopen. I don't think he was lying or just trying to give us some hope. He meant it.

"The granite that came out of that quarry, you know, that was the finest granite anywhere. Grain was perfect, very fine and it polished up like no other, not even the finest they had up in Barre, that's in Vermont, you know. The best was Buckingham. Absolutely the finest and always brought the highest price, which meant it went into only the most expensive buildings." He picked up his Coke and only then did I realize how big his hands were. The bottle almost disappeared. "I never found a gun."

"I found it," I said. "It was under the credenza behind the desk, way up against the back wall."

"It was? Well I wouldn't have looked there, because that's where his body lay. And there was a big pool of dried blood there too. I didn't go near that." He turned and looked directly at me. "But the gun was there, after all. What kind was it?"

"Colt pocket model thirty-two auto."

"Huh. I wonder where that came from. He had a gun in the office because we did a lot of cash business from local masons, but it was a Colt forty-five, single action. Had a seven and a half inch barrel on it. I never saw a thirty-two. Maybe he carried it in his pocket and I never knew."

"Who would have had a reason to kill him?" I asked.

"Now, that's the very question I asked at the time, because, as I told you, I just couldn't see him killing himself. Didn't fit with the man I knew. Could've been a robbery, I suppose. Maybe he walked into the office and surprised someone. He always came in the back door, so he'd have been close to his desk."

"Did you ever hear him argue with anyone?"

"Not a soul."

"How did he act when he announced the closing?" I asked.

"Almost like he was relieved. I suppose it had been weighing on him. Business for the previous six months had slowed to a trickle. He'd kept the men busy building an inventory of the most popular sizes of blocks, but the yard got so full you couldn't move the machinery around."

He sat silently for a while, looking off across the room, his eyes unfocused as he ran back through his memory.

"Only odd thing I remember was a shiny mark on one of the big hinges on the door into his office that I hadn't noticed before. But at the time there was so much else to think about that I forgot it. Days later I remembered but by then it was over. Mr. Batterston had been buried and I'd already signed up for the Navy. Had to. It meant some income and my folks still had three young children at home and I had to do something to help. What I didn't like was the whole cover-up. The family offered me a lot of money, well for the time, a lot of money, and during the Depression everyone needed cash. It didn't make much difference to me. Mr. Batterson was dead and if the police were willing to cover it up, I decided not to rock the boat.

"From time to time I've thought about that day, and sometimes when I'd be up on the bridge on those long nights at sea, before I went to flight school, I'd wonder what could have made that mark. Never could figure it out. Must have been something metal that someone had carried through the door and misjudged the width. Best I could ever come up with."

He finished his Coke and we finished ours.

"What is it you've got in mind here?" he asked.

I shrugged. "I'm not really sure. When I was in the office I thought something was out of place. But if you think about it, that's kind of crazy because I'd never been in there before. Mostly, I wanted to know what happened and who had died there."

"How'd you know anyone had?" Mr. Waverly asked.

"The dark stain on the floor and then the pistol."

He grinned around at his grandson. "He always this sharp?"

"Gramps, you have no idea. Being friends with Cam means things never go where you think they will. You ought to see him on the lacrosse field. He knows what's gonna happen way before it happens."

"Must be my Indian blood," I said.

"You've got Indian blood?" Jack's jaw dropped.

"I'm one-sixteenth Pequot."

"Well," Mr. Waverly said, "explains why you play lacrosse."

I smiled. "Maybe it does. But my dad played in college at Johns Hopkins and I grew up with a lacrosse stick in my hands."

"Used to be an Indian lived here. Billy Owens. Fished the river. Caught sturgeon. Did odd jobs around. Full-blooded Pequot. He worked for the Batterstons quite a bit, as well as for the other wealthy families. I fished and hunted with him most all the time. Very quiet. Never said much. I remember my mother getting on me about hanging out with an Indian. People were a lot more prejudiced then, but I think it was mostly because he was so poor. But I'll tell you this. He knew how to catch fish and he got paid a lot of money for those sturgeon eggs. He figured out how to turn the raw eggs into caviar and the tobacco barons couldn't get enough of 'em."

"What happened to him, Gramps?" Jack asked.

"Lost in the war, so I heard. Somewhere in Germany, they said. Notice was in the paper. Right close to the end, just before the Germans surrendered."

He shook his head. "Haven't thought of Billy Owens for a long, long time. We were close, we were. Hunted together all the time." He grinned. "Caroused a bit too, like all young men. Had some close scrapes there, all right. Between that and the wardens, we stayed pretty busy, just to keep from getting caught."

He looked around at Jack. "I'm sure your father's heard the stories, but don't say anything to your mother. I don't want to hear about setting a bad example."

"Did you know Harry and George Batterston?" I asked.

"Sure I did. Small town then, you know, but they went off to a private school, Hotchkiss, I think it was. We were on the riffraff side of the fence." He grinned again. "To tell you the truth I liked it better there. Didn't have to dress up all the time."

We both grinned. I understood. My family came from a pretty similar background.

"What were his sons like?" I asked.

"Looked down their noses at us, mostly, which didn't bother me or Billy. There was a lot of that then, with the big tobacco families and all. Just a bunch of wealthy snobs, looked down on everyone. But not Mr. Batterston. He was a regular sort."

"So you still think he was murdered?" I asked.

"Not the sort to kill himself."

"Then we need to find out who killed him?"

Mr. Waverly pulled himself to the edge of his chair. "You know, now that I think of it, there were a couple of men who came to see him every month. Always closed the office door. They wore suits and ties and they were gruff, and not terribly polite. I guess if I were to characterize them, I'd say they were gangsters of some kind. Always carried a portmanteau, s'what we called it then. Kind of like a leather gym bag. Once a month like clockwork." He shook his head. "Funny, I'd never thought about that until now. But in those days we had no idea what a gangster looked like. Not until they made movies about them did we know much, and that was after the war." He picked up his empty Coke bottle, shook it, and set it back onto the table. "Let me see what else I might remember." He chuckled. "Wheels don't turn as fast as they did once, but by golly, they still turn pretty good."

12... ON THE RIVER

We were on the river the next morning before light, heading for the pike fishing grounds. Lance was driving the boat and Dad and I were sitting in the stern drinking coffee and watching the sky lighten in the east.

It's impossible to talk when the boat is underway because of the rushing wind and the engines, so I waited until we had got to our pike hole, rigged the rods, and began trolling.

"Did you ever hear of a guy named Billy Owens?"

"Sure! Where'd you hear about him?"

"Jack's grandfather. He fished and hunted with him."

"Not surprised. Bert Waverly probably knew every trout in town by name. And he was a tremendous hunter too, as was Billy Owens. Story goes that everyone thought there were no more deer left in town, but every fall Billy and Bert got deer. And the two of them were a couple of lady killers and hard drinkers. Some said it was a good thing they got out of town when they did before some angry husband went gunning for them."

I laughed. "Are you sure we're talking about the same Bert Waverly?"

"He may not look it now, but I guess in his prime he was a piece of work. Only man in town to win the Congressional Medal of Honor. Dad says that in the first parade they held, the year after the war, all the veterans marched and Bert led the parade. He had row after row of medals and, of course, he was a full commander and he was pretty tall and he pretty much set all those female hearts to twittering." He laughed.

"But when he came back there was no more of the carrying on he'd done before. Went up to Worcester Poly and got his engineering degree and went to work at Pratt. He married Millie Banks and that was that." He sipped his coffee. "Still fished a lot, served several terms as first selectman. People said he'd sowed his wild oats and settled down. You know, I wonder if he gets to go fishing anymore. Maybe we ought to see if he'd like to go out with us sometime."

"And Billy Owens was killed in the war."

Dad nodded. "That's the story." He shook his head. "When the casinos were just getting going I consulted with them a couple of times on how they would handle their money when it began to come in. I was at a meeting one time and there was an old man there. Everyone seemed to treat him with great reverence. His name was Red Eagle and he was the tribal shaman. I don't know why, but I got the idea that he was Billy Owens.

"Just foolishness from listening to the stories the old men told when they thought the women weren't listening." He laughed. "Heck, I wasn't even born then. I never even saw a picture of him."

"Hey," Lance said. "You guys need to concentrate on the fishing."

We both laughed. "That never works," Dad said. " I never

caught a fish when I was thinking about catching a fish."

But suddenly neither of us could think of anything to say so we sat back in our seats and looked out over the river and the countryside. The Connecticut is an unusual river, especially for the Northeast. There are only occasional houses and few of those are close to the water because of the marshes which flood every spring. At times you think you're in wilderness country.

When you're trolling and the fish aren't hitting, you get long stretches of time. There's time to think and I certainly had plenty to think about.

I finished my cup of coffee and looked over at Dad. "Jack's playing lacrosse," I said.

"What brought that on?"

"He got tired of swimming laps. Remember when we played in the youth league?"

"He was pretty darn good as I recall."

"I think he's gonna be great now."

"Doesn't surprise me. Both his father and grandfather were gifted ballplayers." He took a swallow of coffee. "Have you thought any more about what might have happened in the Buckingham Granite office?"

I nodded. "Jack and I talked with our chemistry teacher, Mr. Canfield, about getting some chemicals to test the dark spot on the floor and it turns out he's been studying forensic stuff for years. Tomorrow, he's going with us."

"Sounds like fun."

"I think so."

"Canfield's the smartest teacher in the school," Dad said. "He did his bachelor's at Williams and his master's at MIT."

"Whoa, I sure didn't know that."

"How is he as a teacher?"

"The best. His explains things clearly and he's fair. He's a little weird looking, but you forget that. Do you know him?"

"Small town."

"Not that small."

"I was on a committee to improve the science curriculum and he was the faculty representative. After he gave a talk on where the curriculum was and where it ought to go, I got out of the way. What puzzled me was why he ended up teaching in a high school. With his background he could have made a lot of money."

"Well, I'm glad he didn't," I said.

Just then Dad's rod bent and he grabbed it out of the holder while Lance and I reeled in. It was a big fish and because he had on a deep-running lure we now knew where the fish were.

Lance kept the engines in neutral, letting the boat run with the slow current and Dad played the fish like the expert he is, never allowing any slack line, always keeping his rod tip up, laughing with delight when the fish ran or sounded, heading for deeper water. He might be a very successful hedge fund manager, but when he's fishing, he focuses entirely on fishing, which probably explains his success in business. He concentrates.

Not until he had drawn the fish in close to the boat did we get a look. It was a big old striper, probably a cow on her way back downstream after spawning. Usually those fish don't have a lot of energy left, but from the fight she'd put up, I figured she must have found a couple of schools of hickory shad to feed on because she had plenty of spunk.

But she was also up against a guy who'd caught more striped bass than I could count, and he was patient. He took his time, feeling the fish on the end of the line and knowing what she was

QUARRY

doing and even how much energy she had left. Bit by bit he wore her down and then eased her in close and I reached over, clamped onto her jaw, and pulled her up into the air alongside the boat.

It was a struggle but I finally got her up high enough to get an accurate reading on the scale. Fifty-two pounds. That might sound like a lot to lift, but I curl a hundred.

"All right, Dad!" Lance shouted.

Lance took several pictures and then I lowered the big striper back into the water and held her there to make sure she was okay. For a minute or two she just hung by the boat, pumping water through her gills and then she began to twitch her tail and she eased away from the boat as if she were getting her bearings. Then she swiped her big tail and shot off into the river.

"Did you see how sleek she looked?" I asked.

"Her sides were flat so she must have spawned," Dad said, "but most likely a while ago. Probably got into a school of shad."

It's always nice, I thought, to know you're on the same page as your father. "I hope the stripers don't get them all," I said.

"Maybe we ought to keep more stripers," Dad said.

"That's a lot of fish to eat," Lance said.

He prefers steak, rare, raw in the middle. Blood meat for blood sports is the way he says it. If you saw him on the football field, you'd understand. Quarterbacks live in mortal fear when they have to play us.

We let the lines back out. "You want me to run the boat for awhile, Lance?" I asked.

He grinned around at me. "No, that's okay."

I settled back into the seat, propped my feet on the gunwale and thought about what tomorrow might produce. All in all it was turning out to be a pretty exciting spring.

13... GUNFIGHT

I knew when Jack and I climbed out of the car at the quarry that something had changed. I don't know why such an idea should have occurred to me, but it did and it was strong. I could smell a faint odor which I thought smelled just a little like gunpowder. Then the wind shifted and I could smell only the woods and the water.

Carrying our big cups of Dunkin' Donuts coffee, we walked over to the edge of the quarry at the landing and looked down into the absolutely clear water. I always look into the water. It's what a fisherman does.

Then I let my eyes wander along the edge of the quarry. It's an instinct with anyone who hunts. You check the edges of where the woods give way to open ground because everything hides in the edges.

"You know what I need?" Jack said. "I need a new girlfriend."

"What?"

"This thing with Janelle just isn't working out."

"What brought this on? You two have been an item since

sophomore year."

He shrugged. "I feel like I'm tied down."

"Well, duh, that's what it means when you go out with the same girl for a long time."

"Yeah, yeah, I know." He took a long swallow of coffee. "I think I'm gonna break it off."

"No way."

"I feel like I'm in a corral."

"Did she do something?"

I walked to the right so I could see around the wall of the quarry to where the cars had been pushed over the edge.

"Nothing that I can think of. It's more like little things. Sometimes I think I'm nothing more than a trained dog."

"Whoa, that's ugly," I said.

"Totally nasty," Jack said, "totally. I think I've been walking in ruts, you know?"

"That why you wanted to play lacrosse?"

"Could be part of it."

"She say anything about that?"

"She doesn't like it."

"What's with that?"

"I think it took her by surprise."

"Yeah, well, there could be something in that."

"She doesn't like surprises unless there's a present."

"How about we talk about something else. I'm kind of out of my element here."

"Who isn't?"

I stopped and lifted my head into the wind, catching a whiff of what now I knew was gunpowder.

"What?" Jack asked.

"I smell gunpowder."

"Is this one of those things like you always do?"

I nodded and looked up to the spot where the cars had gone into the water and then I looked down to the water.

"Uh-oh," I said.

"Uh-oh? Is this a big uh-oh, or a little uh-oh?"

I pointed to the water below the ledge. "See that?"

"What?"

"Bubbles. Lots and lots of bubbles like there's something on the bottom that wasn't there a while ago. Like maybe another car."

"How random is that?" Jack said. "We're here both times?"

"Heck of a coincidence."

Just then two men stepped out from behind the trees, walked to the edge, and looked over. Not until they turned did they spot us, then they ran back into the woods. We heard a car start up and tear off.

"So I'm guessing a really, really, big uh-oh. Would that be about right?" Jack asked.

I already had my cell phone out and I punched in the number Tom had given me.

"Tom?"

"Yeah?"

"This is Cam. Jack and I are up at the quarry and somebody just pushed another car off the ledge!"

"Hang where you are. I'll be there in a couple of minutes. Did you get a look at 'em?"

"I did."

"Have they gone?"

"I heard a car start up and go tearing off."

QUARRY

"Okay." I heard his truck start and then heard his tires screech as he started forward. "Do you think they can identify you?"

"They got a good look. Is that a problem?"

"I'm on my way. Hide somewhere. I gotta make a couple of calls."

"Okay."

"What's your guess?" Jack asked. "Another body?"

"We need to find cover."

"Hey," Jack laughed. "I know this drill."

I looked around and I pointed to the woods. "Let's go. Keep low and run!"

In seconds we were out of sight. I picked a low rise covered by a dense growth of young pine and I pushed into the thick copse and sat down. Jack followed.

"What's this all about?"

I whispered. "Keep still. Wait 'til Tom gets here."

We waited like what seemed an hour but it was no more than six minutes before Tom came roaring up the road in his truck. I got up and signalled for Jack to follow me. We eased back down toward the landing, staying behind big solid trees until we could look out.

He swung the truck so that the passenger side was toward the high ground, then slid out, keeping low.

My cell phone vibrated and I opened it. "Yeah?"

"Cam, you here?" he said into his cell phone.

"Back here. In the pines. We're coming out."

There were no waves on the surface of the water, which meant the car had gone in some time ago, but the bubbles were still rising steadily. Tom moved away from the truck and turned toward us, managing, I thought, never to expose himself long enough for anyone to have gotten off an accurate shot. He was dressed in jeans and a sweatshirt.

"How did you guys happen to be here?" he asked.

"I'll tell you later. It's kind of complicated."

"You think they've gone?" Tom asked.

"Something's not right," I said.

He looked at me, stared at me, and then nodded. "You think there's more?"

I nodded. "A lot more."

"Like what?"

"I don't know. It just feels like it isn't over."

"And I can trust your instincts here?"

"You should," Jack said. "He does things like this, he has since he was a kid. He told me before he could smell gunpowder."

"Okay." Tom drew his Colt forty-five from behind his back. "I'm gonna look around. You guys just keep your heads down."

We moved back behind the pile of granite blocks and watched Tom, moving off into the woods like a ghost. He was a hunter and he moved silently, using the trunks of trees for cover, and I thought he'd been trained for something a lot more desperate than hunting.

It couldn't have taken more than a few minutes before I heard him shout. "Police! Put your guns down and your hands on your head."

What followed was gunfire, maybe nine millimeter, and then Tom's forty-five boomed four times and it was quiet. We waited and after several minutes Tom appeared on the ridge and started down toward us.

"Took 'em by surprise," he said as he came up to us.

"Did you kill 'em?" Jack asked. He looked like he'd just walked into a wall.

"Two of them. I think they were left behind to clean up the witnesses they hadn't expected. One of them had a sniper rifle."

I shook my head, stunned at how close we'd come to getting wasted. "Got any idea who they are?"

"Mob guys. Probably from Providence. Place is crawling with guys like that." He looked around at me. "We had a guy in my outfit in Afghanistan who knew when things were gonna happen. He kept us alive. We could never figure out how he did that. Do you know how you do it?"

I shook my head. "I always know when people are watching me, but there's something more, kind of like a premonition."

"You use that on the lacrosse field, don't you?"

I grinned. "My mother says I've got eyes in the back of my head."

"And that's a good thing," Tom said.

In the distance we could hear the sirens and then we heard a car and Mr. Canfield drove in, parked, and climbed out.

"Hey, Bob," Tom called. "What brings you up here?"

It was time for explanations.

I told Tom what I had found in the office and that I had taken the pistol home and Dad had locked it up in the gun safe. Then I told him why Mr. Canfield was there.

He shook his head and grinned. "Kind of a busy place."

A state police cruiser pulled up into the loading area and stopped.

We walked over to the cruiser and as the trooper climbed out, Tom showed him his badge and then explained what had happened.

"Everyone's okay?" the trooper asked.

"Except for the two dead guys up on the ridge."

"Let me make a call then we'll take a walk up there."

Mr. Canfield was looking a little strange. His face had turned kind of gray and I wondered what that was all about.

"You okay?" I asked.

"Yes, yes, just a little more excitement than I'm used to. I don't see a lot of this in my chemistry classes."

"We're gonna be looking at two dead guys, you ready for that?" Tom asked.

"Oh, yes. That won't bother me at all. I've watched a dozen autopsies."

Tom looked around at me. "You think there are more?"

I nodded. "There's something but I don't know what."

The state trooper looked at me like he was seeing me for the first time and then he looked back at Tom.

Tom grinned. "He knows things," he said. "I'd have walked right into those two guys waiting up on the ridge if Cam hadn't warned me. Now, I ask and I listen."

The trooper nodded. "I knew a guy in Iraq who did that."

It made me feel a whole lot better to have two guys up front who had seen actual battle. And then I stopped and looked out through the trees to the far edge of the quarry across from us where I'd walked before. The ground there was in bright sunlight and I scanned it and then moved forward a step or two, dodging some branches and scanned again.

"What are you looking at?" Jack asked.

"Just looking." What I didn't tell him was that all the time I'd spent hunting in the woods had taught me to be aware of things that didn't fit, movement where it didn't belong, colors out of place. It's how you see deer before they know you're there.

QUARRY

"Everybody down!" I said in a harsh whisper and we all hit the ground. Speaking softly, I said, "there's a guy on the ridge across the quarry. He's dressed in full camo. Even his face is painted. He's got a rifle and I think he was looking for a hole to shoot through."

We waited.

"Still see him?" Tom asked.

"He's there. He hasn't moved."

"Show me."

"There's a big boulder and just to the east a small clump of hemlock. He's in there, maybe six feet inside the trees. When the wind blows it moves the trees and the sun glances off his scope."

"Yeah, okay," Tom said, "I got him." He rolled onto his side. "Everyone wait here. Stay down, find a rock to get behind and crawl to it."

Tom takes aim.

"What are you planning?" the trooper asked.

"I told you that one of the guys I shot had a sniper rifle. Maybe I can even things up some."

"You can't just shoot him," the trooper said. "You don't even know what he's doing there."

"I plan to find that out. Just keep low."

Tom crawled off and I knew he didn't have far to go, but whatever he was planning took some time. When it happened it was quick. The guy with the rifle slipped the gun to his shoulder and fired and a millisecond later Tom fired and the guy slumped forward, rolled out onto the rock and over the edge and into the quarry.

"My God!" Mr. Canfield said.

We jumped up and ran to the top and there was Tom, holding the rifle and one of the guys he had shot before was slumped forward at the base of a big pine wearing Tom's sweatshirt.

The trooper shook his head. "Guess there wasn't much doubt."

"None," Tom said.

"Too bad you had to waste that sweatshirt," the trooper said.

Tom grinned. "I always liked that sweatshirt."

The trooper looked across the quarry. "What's that, three hundred yards?"

"Three seventy-five," Tom said.

"Where'd you learn to do that?"

"Afghanistan."

"Sniper?"

Tom nodded.

"I loved it when we had snipers with us. Saved a lot of soldiers."

QUARRY

"We seemed to make everyone around us kind of nervous. It's the cold-blooded thing."

The trooper nodded. Then he stepped forward and looked at the bodies, noting the holes in the guy who had Tom's shirt on. "Looks like you're pretty good with a pistol too."

"Army champion," I said.

"How'd you know that?" Tom asked.

"My Dad."

"Your father has a knack for knowing things."

I nodded. "Makes it tough being his kid sometimes."

Everyone laughed except Jack. He was way too pumped up. Well, we all were. You don't go through a thing like that without quarts of adrenalin and testosterone flooding your system. And once you've experienced that, it can get addictive. I felt it every time we played a game.

The next couple of hours were given over to police routine. They called in the Medical Examiner, the dive team and Mr. Hulm and his big wrecker.

For a while Tom filled out paperwork and talked to the state homicide detectives and we watched them haul the car out of the quarry. As we had expected, there was another body.

Then, as things wound down, Tom took us off to the side. "How'd you guys like to show me the office? Maybe I'll get to work a murder case for once."

14... Digging Deeper

If it hadn't been for daylight savings time we wouldn't have had enough light to check out the office because it had taken a while to haul out the car with its fresh body and then tie up all the loose ends that go with any murder investigation and, of course, they also had to haul the other body out of the quarry and load up the two guys on the ridge.

I opened the door with the key, explaining why I had it, and once we were inside I explained what I had found, pointing out the dates on the paper work and the outline in the dust where I had found the pistol.

Then, while Mr. Canfield opened his satchel and prepared to test the dark stains on the floor and Tom began poking into things, Jack and I walked into the outer office to start looking through the file cabinets.

We'd been at it a while when Mr. Canfield stepped into the room. "Well, there's blood all over the place, behind the desk on the floor and on the wall by the door. Judging by the size of the stain and the position of the stain and the splatter pattern of the blood, I'd say that the victim was close to the floor when he was shot. Most likely sitting. There's a hole through the floor at the edge of the credenza, and my guess would be that we'll find the bullet in the basement."

"There's a strongbox in the floor of the closet," Tom said. "It's been pried open. There was nothing left inside. From where I stand that looks like a motive for armed robbery."

In the bright westerly light from the sun, something caught my eye and I stepped around Mr. Canfield and walked over to the door.

Just as Mr. Waverly had said there was a mark on the top hinge. It ran diagonally and I stepped back, made a line with my eye, and discovered I was looking at the ceiling in the outer room.

"What are you looking for?" Jack asked.

"Remember your grandfather told us about a mark on the door hinge? Well, I thought maybe that mark had been made by a bullet." I pointed to the hinge. The mark is here, just as he said, and it runs in a diagonal, pointing toward the ceiling over there."

The groove was shallow and in normal light might have been all but invisible but now it showed clearly. I moved one of the chairs over, climbed up and examined the cut in the plaster.

The bullet had come in at a shallow angle and I thought there was a good chance it hadn't gone on through into the attic.

I stepped down off the chair. "Time to bring in the expert." I turned. "Tom, I found a mark in the ceiling out here and it looks like it was made by a bullet."

He walked out into the room, with Mr. Canfield right behind him.

"It is a bullet," Mr. Canfield said. "There's blood on the door frame and a mark on the door hinge." He walked right to where I had spotted the groove, turned toward me and smiled. "Right where you said, Cam."

Tom climbed up onto the chair, pulled out a Leatherman knife, and dug around in the hole. Then he closed the blade, opened the pliers, and extracted a small bullet. He dropped it into the palm of his hand and looked around at me. It was mashed up on one side but the rest of it was intact.

Mr. Canfield looked down at the bullet. "We'll need to test it, but it looks like there's a blood stain all right."

Tom handed it to him and Mr. Canfield took it back to where he had set up his test kit and we watched him pour the chemical over the solid lead bullet and then turn his ultra-violet light on it. The blood glowed in the light.

Mr. Canfield pointed toward the wall to the right of the door to the front office. "From the splatters on the wall and the height of the hinge, it seems probable that he was standing just inside the door of the room, and based on the damage to the bullet, which seems to have come mostly from the hinge and the ceiling he only had a flesh wound." He paused and rubbed his chin.

"I think that the victim was sitting on the floor behind the desk, which would indicate there had been a struggle and the shooter knocked him down. Then the victim drew his gun and fired and the other man shot back. Which brings me to another point. I need to find the bullet that went through the floor. From the size of the stain I would say it was a substantial wound, most likely caused by at least a thirty-eight caliber bullet, though maybe something as large as a forty-four or forty-five. Of course, the corpse would show us that, but somehow I don't think Dr. Batterston will agree to an exhumation."

QUARRY

"Be my guess," Tom said. "What else can you tell us?"

"The man at the desk was left handed, or at least that's the hand he used to hold his pistol. If he were right handed, sitting where he was, the angle would have been different and his view would not have been partially blocked by the desk. More likely, he would have hit his target and the bullet would have produced a good deal more than a flesh wound."

"There's a cellar door outside," I said.

Tom nodded. "Let's go take a look."

The building had been built into a shallow hill, the foundation made of mortared granite blocks. There was also a chimney I hadn't noticed before, probably because most buildings have chimneys.

The door was a single slab of granite with a great iron latch handle and release bar fastened with a lock designed for a skeleton type key like the one in the back door. I took out my oil, squirted it into the lock and followed it with the key, reasoning that the key would fit, because nobody wanted to carry around many of those big old keys.

"You always carry a bottle of oil?" Tom asked.

"Never know what'll come up," I said.

"You're a piece of work, Cam, you know that?"

"Yeah, that's pretty much always been the case."

"He keeps it hidden, though," Jack said. "Otherwise nobody'd talk to him."

I kept working the key back and forth in the lock and suddenly it turned the tumblers and I lifted the latch and pushed inward. The hinges squealed like badly frightened little girls, but the weight of the door overcame the rust and I took out my small light and stepped through the doorway.

Tom had his light on and Mr. Canfield also carried a light and with the three lights we got a good look at the inside of the room. It was built like a tomb. The walls were granite, the floor was granite, all the pieces carefully matched and perfectly fitted together. There was no smell of mildew, just the odor of dead air which began to sweeten quickly.

In one corner stood a big old furnace and a bin full of hard coal. Along one wall there was a tall wooden cabinet and, as Tom and Mr. Canfield began looking for the bullet, Jack and I checked out the cabinet. I opened the double doors. Shoeboxes. White shoeboxes with labels denoting style and size. I pulled one out and opened it to find a bottle full of very clear liquid with a cork stopper.

"Tom," I called, "is this what I think it is?"

He walked over, took the bottle and held it up. He took out his Swiss Army knife, opened the corkscrew and pulled the cork from the bottle. He sniffed it and then held it out for me to smell. "Gin," he said. "How many bottles are there?"

"One hundred and forty-five," Jack said.

"Is this where the shoe guy got his gin?" I asked.

Tom shook his head and grinned. "How do you know about that?"

"Stuff you pick up."

"To answer your question, I don't think so. There's not enough here for that. Most likely Mr. Batterston kept his private stash here and brought it down to the house when he needed it." He scratched his head. "The next question is where he got it from?"

"I found the bullet," Mr. Canfield said as he crossed the base-ment and held out his open hand to display a badly mashed bul-

QUARRY

let. "Forty-five Long Colt, most likely. And it does have traces of blood on it." He looked at the bottle in Tom's hand and then at the cabinet. "Well, my golly, it was true. White shoes, brown shoes. I always thought it was just a story."

Tom handed him the bottle and he smelled it, blew through his nose and sniffed it again. "This is a very high quality gin. About eighty-six proof with an especially nice mix of juniper berries. Whoever made this knew what he was doing."

"You can tell that from the odor?" I asked.

"Oh, absolutely. I'm a chemist, you know." He grinned. "But I was also born with an exceptional sense of smell. Local wineries call me all the time to check their new wines."

"There's something you should know about this," Jack said. "It came from my grandfather. The family said Mr. Batterston died of a heart attack but that wasn't true. My grandfather found the body. He was the office boy. He said Mr. Batterston had been shot in the head."

"With a large caliber round." I said.

"He said the hole was big enough for a forty-five and there was a lot of blood."

"That supports my theory," Mr. Canfield said.

"He also said that Mr. Batterston had a forty-five Colt with a long barrel," Jack said.

"But why did they cover it up?" Mr. Canfield asked.

"My grandfather was sworn to secrecy and they even paid him off. He said he guessed it wouldn't hurt for the truth to come out now," Jack said.

"What else did he say?" Tom asked.

"Not much but he said he'd see what else he could remember." He looked around at me. "I'm guessing Cam and I will be

119

visiting him again."

"You think?" I said.

"That still supports the theory of an armed robbery," Tom said. "The guy knew about the gin and then he found the forty-five. Batterston must have had the thirty-two in his pocket." He looked at his watch. "Time for me to get back to headquarters. I'll be in touch."

"I have to go along as well," Mr. Canfield said.

Jack and I watched them go.

"This is awesome!" Jack said.

"Yeah, it is."

"What next?"

"Let's go back upstairs and have a look at those file cabinets. I'll take the cabinets in the back office and you take the ones out front."

"What am I looking for?"

"Basically, something that either doesn't seem to fit or something that might have led to trouble with someone."

"Whoa, that's a little broad, don't you think?"

I nodded. "But it's a place to start."

The two file cabinets in Mr. Batterston's office were four drawers high and I opened the top drawer of the cabinet on the left, marked A-C. It seemed reasonable to assume that whatever had happened had been recent so I only went back two years in each category.

The last two years' files were very thin and they got thicker as I went back and I guessed that was because business had been better then.

It was pretty dull stuff: invoices, bills, a smattering of business letters. I'd nearly finished when I heard Jack call.

QUARRY

"Hey, I'm falling asleep out here. I'm thinking I should have a pile of these next to my bed to put me to sleep at night."

I laughed, closed the last drawer, and walked into the outer office.

"It was worth a try, and look at how much you learned about the granite business."

"If it isn't gonna be on a test I don't need it."

"I tell you what. Before it gets any darker in here, start looking around for anything that might be hidden."

"You mean like the safe was hidden?"

"Yeah."

I went back into Mr. Batterston's office and sat down in the chair behind the desk. It felt weird but from that position I could look around the office and see things the way he had. There wasn't much to see, nothing on the walls, nothing to divert your attention. It made me think he had been a man who focused on his business. The chair creaked softly as I let it lean back and because it went so far my knees came up against the underside of the desktop. It moved.

I sat back up, took hold of the top and tried to lift it, but though it moved, it stayed put. Here's the thing. Desktops do not move. They are screwed in place. I took hold of the top and pushed to the left and then to the right and suddenly it swung back toward me, revealing a large area about an inch deep and it was filled with papers and letters. I felt as if I'd struck gold.

I gathered the papers, stacked them, and closed the desk. Then I walked into the outer office

"You found something?"

"I found some papers he didn't want anyone else to know about."

"Where were they?"

"Secret compartment in the desk. Let's go. It'll be dusk soon and for some reason I don't want to be hanging out here when it gets dark."

"Good call," Jack said.

We went out the back, locked the door, walked over to the car, and climbed in. I stuck the key into the ignition and suddenly Jack stopped me.

"What?"

"We need to check under the car," he said.

I laughed. "For what? A bomb?"

He nodded.

"You've been watching too many mafia movies," I said.

"Who's dumping bodies in the quarry? How many mob guys got whacked this afternoon?"

Slowly, I pulled the key from the ignition, opened the glove compartment and took out the flashlight. "Let's have a look."

There was nothing under the hood and Jack took the light and, lying on his back, stuck his head under the car and shone the light around.

He slid out from under the car. "You'd better call Tom and see if they've got a bomb squad."

"No way ..."

"It's hooked to the tie rods and I think it's designed to go off when the car gets to a certain speed. And if what I see in the movies is accurate, this is a really big bomb."

15... NEW DIRECTION

That old road probably hadn't seen so much police activity since it was first cut through. This time, however, we didn't get to stand around and watch. They evacuated us a mile down the road and while we waited we called home to check in and said we'd explain when we got there.

It took an hour and a half before they allowed us back to get the car. The bomb squad hadn't left and when I asked, the leader of the squad showed us the device and explained.

"There is enough C-4 here to have shredded your car. It was set to detonate when your car hit forty miles an hour." He shook his head and unfastened the upper part of his protective suit. "Had there been any houses nearby when it detonated it might well have flattened them. I've defused a number of bombs but never anything this big or this sophisticated." He dropped the heavy jacket on the floor of the van. "Absolutely professional."

He picked up a strange looking device with a roller on one end. "The way it worked, this roller was positioned to contact the wheel and it was connected to a device that read the speed of the wheel." He tossed it upward and caught it. "I don't know who's after you, but my advice is to get some help and get it fast." He nodded toward another man. "The Captain will want to talk to you and your families."

Scared? Well, try terrified. I looked at Jack and he looked as if he'd just been told the world was coming to an end and I know I didn't look any different. But I was also impressed that Jack had figured out how the bomb was designed to work.

What we needed to know was who had placed the bomb under my car. As far as we knew, the mafia guys had all been up on the ridge. But maybe the first guys hadn't really left. Knowing which direction the police would come from, they could have parked down the road, sneaked back, and rigged the bomb. It was the only logical explanation. No. There was one other. The sniper would have had time.

Both families met at our house with Tom and Captain Waxman of the State Police and he explained how the bomb had been rigged and how dangerous it was.

A tall man, in his fifties, his close cropped brown hair just beginning to gray, he spoke softly and carefully and we understood that we were in the middle of something big and dangerous.

"This won't be in the papers," he said. "We want them to think that the bomb didn't work and leave them guessing. So far we have no suspects and not much to go on. Sometimes these guys use outside contractors for bomb work. The FBI and the BATF are investigating because anything to do with explosives brings them in. They'll trace all the parts of the bomb, but they won't get far. The guy was a pro and he knows how the feds work."

"It doesn't make sense," I said. "If they were trying to wipe us out because of what we saw, the bomb had to have been set after they pushed the car into the quarry. That means they had to have the stuff with them. Would they have had a bomb guy along?"

Captain Waxman shook his head. "You make a good point. I'll go over the timing with the bomb experts. Maybe we'll have to spread a wider net."

"By not going public," Dad said, "you're essentially using the boys as bait."

Captain Waxman nodded. "When nothing turns up in the press or on the TV, the guys who put the bomb there will know that we found the bomb and we're gonna be on full alert."

"Are you sure of that?" Dad asked.

He shook his head slowly, looking down at the floor and then slowly back up at us. "No. "

Dad nodded. "But the guys upstairs figure that if they admit the threat still exists, then they might have to offer us protection and they haven't got money in the budget for that."

"That about sums it up."

Jack's mother was not taking this well at all. "Do you know how crazy that is?"

"If anything happens, do you know how big the lawsuit is going to be?" Dad asked.

"They know. I told them. They may reconsider after I talk to them again. I expect we'll have some legal people there too."

"What are we supposed to do in the meantime?" Mrs. Waverly asked. "Hire a security service?"

He stood up. "I'm sorry I can't offer more just now, but I will be working on it. Between us and the feds we've got a lot of people on this. Word will get back to the boys in Providence and they are going to disappear for some time."

"Maybe," Dad said, "you could tell me just why I pay taxes?"

"If you figure that out, let me know," Captain Waxman said. "I'll e-mail some photos of possible suspects as soon as I get back to the barracks."

At first, we all sat there in the living room saying nothing and if I had thought that bomb had looked dangerous it was nothing to how I felt about the way Dad and Mr. Waverly looked.

"I'm gonna get something to eat," I said and headed for the kitchen with Lance and Jack and Jack's brother Jason following me. It was time to leave the adults alone.

I got out some cold cuts and bread and mayo and Cokes and chips and we dug in. Jack's brother is only ten, but he's a good guy and a lot like his brother, except that he's not a swimmer and he doesn't play lacrosse ... yet.

"Lance, why don't you show Jason your latest X-Box games," I said.

"Cool," he said, picking up his sandwich, chips, and soda.

"Great!" Jason said as they headed for the den.

Jack and I concentrated on eating and then I sat back in my chair and looked over at him. "Do you think Batterston's death could have anything to do with this?"

He shrugged. "Maybe we should look at those papers."

"Good call." I stood up. "They're in my room."

Upstairs, I closed the door, handed Jack a bunch of the papers and he sat in the easy chair and I sat on my bed.

Unlike what we had found in the file cabinets, this was not the least bit dull. In fact it was astonishing, if I was understanding what I read.

"I'm not sure what to make of this," Jack said.

"Maybe I'm wrong, but the way I'm reading this, Mr.

QUARRY

Batterston was a major bootlegger during Prohibition. And now I'm gonna bet that the gin we found in that cabinet was something he made."

"What exactly was Prohibition?"

The question took me considerably by surprise. "You really don't know?"

"I never even heard of it."

"The country banned booze. They voted to amend the Constitution."

"You mean like alcohol? Beer? Wine? They did that?"

"It put the mafia in business."

"How do you know this?"

"I read a lot, remember?"

"Okay, I'm catching on. Somehow, they got the booze and distributed it. But who bought it?"

"It went to private clubs called speakeasies. There was a guy here in town who used to run a dry goods store and he sold it: white shoes for gin and brown shoes for whiskey."

He laughed. "That's what that was all about in the cellar. I didn't know about that."

"Yeah."

"And he never got caught?"

"I think the police were probably paid off. That's usually the way it worked."

"Where did they get the whiskey?"

"A lot of it came from Canada, some from Mexico, and a bunch of people ran stills. That's what Batterston was doing."

"How big is a still?"

"It would have to be pretty big to fill any sort of demand, and if we assume he was a bootlegger, then there would have been a huge demand."

"But where would he have put it?"

I grinned. "Definitely not in the office."

"It's the only building."

Suddenly I had a thought. It was pretty far out, but it seemed like a possibility. "Suppose it was in the quarry."

"Underwater?"

"Sort of. Suppose they cut a big cave back into the rock? If they cut it so it ran uphill, they could let the water cover the entrance without flooding the cave and then pump the water down to get inside. Or maybe there's a back entrance somewhere."

"Why would they have needed an entrance into the quarry then?" Jack asked.

"It would have been easier to cut the rock there because that's where they had the machinery. And besides, if they used another entrance they would have had to build a road and that would have drawn attention."

"Okay, that's logical, I guess." He shook his head. "Naw, it would've been way too much trouble."

"That depends on how big a still they were running."

"Where would they get the supplies they needed to make the stuff?"

"Farmers. And they probably had several trucks so no one would have suspected those trucks were carrying anything but granite."

He grinned. "I'm still not convinced."

"So to speak ..."

"Huh?"

"Still and still?"

"Weak, Cam, really, really weak."

QUARRY

"I wonder if anyone else knows about the cave."

"If there is a cave."

"We need to do some exploring," I said.

"Are you nuts? We've being chased by a mad bomber and his gunmen and you want to go walking around in the woods?"

"Too crazy, huh?"

"Way too crazy."

"Yeah, I guess you're right." I grinned. "But my interview with Dr. Batterston might turn up something new. And remember this. It explains why his father could have been murdered. Remember what your grandfather said about those guys who came every month with a satchel? Maybe those were mob guys and maybe they had a falling out. He probably could've named names. The last dates in the office are December 1936. Prohibition was repealed in December of 1933 and that put him out of the liquor business."

"You know what bothers me?" Jack said. "What bothers me is who attached the bomb to the car."

"I've got the same problem."

"It doesn't make any sense. No way would they have hung around with cops coming from every direction."

"Good point," I said.

"Got any other suspects?"

"The sniper."

"Yeah, you think?"

I looked up. "He had the time."

"But why?"

"I'm working on that part."

"Who's the guy with the dogs, you told me about?"

In a flash my brain began putting it together. If you could

make whiskey in a cave, you could also grow marijuana. All you needed was power for growlights and you could supply that with generators.

"You know you may be onto something here. Maybe they spotted me when I was up in that tree."

"I'm gonna say they did."

"So the thing to do is go have a closer look."

"No. The thing to do is call in the cops. Those guys are probably growing the stuff right there in their barn."

"I'll call Tom."

"I'm gonna say that a bust like that could make his career," Jack said.

"It would."

"So, talk to him and see what he says."

"What can he do? There's no evidence. He can't just go barging in there. He'll need a warrant and without some evidence no judge will give him one."

"How do you know that kinda stuff?"

"It's in the newspapers, it's in the crime shows on TV."

"I don't know about newspapers, but I do know that stuff on the TV is fiction."

"Maybe so, but you can't just go busting into somebody's place without a warrant. That's illegal search and seizure and the Constitution says you can't do that. All I have are guesses."

He scratched his head. "Yeah but ..."

"Look at it this way. Suppose some jerk decided to get you in trouble and all he had to do was go to the cops and make up some story and they came rushing in and found something you weren't supposed to have."

"You get warrants from judges, right? And to get a warrant

from a judge, you have to say why you need it and you'd have to have evidence."

"You got it," I said, but now I knew I had to go look around and it'd be better if I didn't take Jack with me. It was one thing to take the risk myself, but it was unfair to ask that of Jack. I even knew where to start. The graveyard.

"Okay," Jack said, "at the risk of breaking your train of thought, I want to talk about the games we got coming up this week."

"You want to know how much you're gonna play."

"Exactly!"

"A lot."

"You think?"

"You're a little rusty but you're way ahead of anyone else who can play the point, something you probably figured out by now."

"Yeah. That's the way I see it."

"My guess is you'll start and if you screw up, Coach'll pull you."

He nodded. "Fair enough. You can't have screw-ups on the field."

"These are good teams, you know. It won't be like the game you watched last week. They've got mostly seniors and juniors the way we did last year. You, me, and C-Shack are the only seniors on the team. We'll be lucky to lose by no more than three goals."

"I don't do losing," Jack said, and in his voice I heard a level of determination that mirrored the way I feel about losing. Things were definitely looking up, even as, on the other hand, they were not. I have never liked graveyards.

16... ANOTHER TEST

Monday at practice we concentrated on working plays and maintaining focus. I understood. Coach was building up our confidence, getting us ready for Tuesday when we faced Cheshire, which looked like it might just be the best team in the state, even though it was still early in the season. What we knew for sure was that they played mostly upperclassmen and the year before, playing mostly juniors, they had finished second in the state.

I was not feeling terribly confident going into the game with Cheshire because our team was, after all, young. I'd been thinking all along that we were in a rebuilding year, but Coach Bradford in his last words of the day did his best to disabuse us of that notion, telling us flat out that words like "rebuilding" were for teams that didn't have enough talent to win.

"We have an advantage," he said. "They don't know us. Outside of two guys, they haven't ever seen any of you play. They know about Cam and they know about C-Shack and they'll be expecting a strong defense. But we are going to be absolutely relentless on offense. Nobody stops running. What we might lack in game experience, we can make up for with overall team speed and pure energy. You guys are the junkyard dogs, the dogs that take people by surprise. Tomorrow, we show our fangs!"

I loved it and so did the rest of the guys, especially the part about the fangs. Lacrosse is a game that lends itself to that kind of thinking. But what I liked best of all was the notion that we were expected to win because I wanted to graduate a winner.

My hopes hung on Jack and he had been outstanding in Monday's practice. He took charge and he directed the offense and things had come together better than I could have hoped. He was the leader the offense had lacked and as long as he was on the field they came together and their confidence began to grow.

It helped, I think, that Cheshire came into the game expecting to clean our clocks. And for the first quarter they almost did. We scored once, Jack rolling off a screen and firing a rifle of a shot past their goalie.

But in lacrosse one goal is nothing. Everybody expects to give up some goals. What we did was play outstanding defense, especially C-Shack. For a big guy he is quick and he has the ability to see things developing before they do, so he knows where the shot is gonna come from.

Of course his height and his wide body help. He doesn't care whether he gets hit with the ball or not, and I gotta tell you a lacrosse ball is nasty when it's traveling over a hundred miles an hour. It's a hard ball and that speed is about the same as a major league pitcher when he's really on. What that means is, you get hit, it hurts.

But I guess if you play football, getting hit is part of the game and C-Shack used whatever part of his body he could to block the goal, and despite a lot of talented guys on the Cheshire offense, guys who had been playing together for years, they managed only two goals in the first quarter.

Just before we took the field for the second quarter, Jack nudged me. "I'm tired of these guys shutting us down. I'm gonna take it to 'em."

"We could use a little rest on defense," I said. "It'd be good if you could keep the ball on the other end of the field for a while." I grinned. "And goals are another good thing."

He grinned. "We need to score a lot of goals."

We got the ball at the start and Jack was like a wild hungry man chasing meat, running hard, never seeming to stop, carrying the ball past and through the defense, looking for a pass or a shot. He kept the heat on their defense and he only gave up the ball when he had an open man to pass to.

Coach was hollering from the sideline, "SCREEN! SCREEN!"

It was like the offense had never heard the word before or maybe they thought it was something used to keep bugs out ... and then ... suddenly, Kyle woke up. He blew out from behind the goal, using it as a screen, and Jack shot him a pass, broke into the open, took the return pass from Kyle, and fired a low one hopper that shot past the goalie and into the net.

Cheshire got the ball on the face off, but seconds later I picked off a pass and fired the ball upfield. Jack picked it off on the run, faked the defender so hard that his knees buckled, and then faked a shot to get the goalie to move, twisted to his right and unloaded a shot that caught the corner of the goal just under the crossbar.

There is no feeling like being on a team when the adrenalin starts to flow and this was more like a river rushing through

QUARRY

us. We made impossible plays, the kind of plays you only dream about completing. Now, everything was within our reach.

On defense we covered our men, we kept them from getting open for a pass, and then picked off their mistakes and ran until we could find an open man, and at that point we had our choice of open guys because they were getting open, running fakes and screens, picking and rolling and always there was Jack, making life miserable for their defense because they had to double team him and that left more guys open. And when they dropped the double team on Jack, he scored. He played the way I remembered him playing in the youth league. He had been the highest scorer and he had not forgotten how to do that.

At the half we were up six to two and playing like madmen.

Coach Bradford sat us down and walked slowly back and forth, looking at the ground and he made several passes before he stopped in front of us.

"That was as good a period as I have ever seen a team play." He looked at us, taking his time, letting it sink in. "So now you know how well you can play when you're pumped. The question is how well you play when you come off that high, and everyone does. It comes in spurts and then it disappears. When that happens you have to rely on technical skill. You have to execute and you have to think.

"You're playing against a very skilled, athletic bunch of guys and you can expect them to come out in the third quarter with only one thing on their minds. They won't want simply to win. They'll want to blow you off the field and, in truth, they are capable of doing just that.

"But we are not going to just play defense. We are going to attack because attack is what you do in lacrosse. You have to harry them, hassle them, knock 'em down. I don't care if we have to take some penalties. Sometimes it's the only way to get into their heads and let them know that we are not going away.

"The best part is that if you can keep them at bay, if you make everything hard, they are going to get frustrated and as the game gets shorter, they'll begin making penalties."

He clapped his hands together and it sounded like a rifle shot. "Huddle!"

We gathered in a big knot, hands extended, touching.

"Go out there and show these guys just how good you are!"

Man, we tore onto that field. So did Cheshire and what followed was a lesson in lacrosse. At times I thought they had twenty guys on the field. They made incredible passes, the kind you see in a Johns Hopkins game. In any game where the goal is small, the action packs into a smaller and smaller space as play gets close to the goal.

The trenches. That's where I play. I never let them set a screen on me, I roll with the shooter on the pick and roll, my stick up, keeping myself between the shooter and the ball. And the other guys on defense play every bit as hard. That doesn't mean Cheshire didn't get any shots, because they did.

And they scored because there has never been a goalie who could stop every shot that came at him, especially if it comes from up close. Look at it this way, a big league pitcher throwing at a hundred miles an hour is about sixty feet away and not even the best hitters can get a bat on a pitch like that. Try it at ten feet. The ball is simply moving so fast there's no time to react. Even so, C-Shack stopped all but four of them and we went into the final quarter tied.

Almost the entire third quarter had been played at my end

QUARRY

of the field. That had to change. It had taken too much out of us. We were tired and they could see that and we knew what was coming. It would be an all-out assault by their offense.

What they didn't know was that Jack was pissed. He has a lot of his grandfather in him, I think, and he came out slashing and attacking and he kept knocking the ball loose and picking it up, but now our guys on offense were a step slow and he had no one to pass to. What he did was keep the ball in his basket and run. I guess the work on the diving board must have paid off because he had strength in his legs that was hard to believe.

Twice he simply outran the defense and twice he scored.

So did they. Three times and that's the way the game finished: nine to eight. A loss. But it did not feel like a loss, because we came out of that game knowing we were going to win far more matches than we would lose.

How good were we? Hey, when we shook hands at the end of the game, in the eyes of the Cheshire players we saw respect. Nobody had to say a word. Their coach even asked Jack and me where we were going to college in the fall. It was the first time I'd ever been recruited. He wanted us to go to Duke, where he had gone.

In the locker room after we'd showered and dressed, Coach sat us down.

"Today was a good day," he said. He smiled. "Today you learned what no coach can ever teach you. You learned about yourselves and how far you can go when you decide to play." He shook his head, looked down and then back up. "But you're short on conditioning. You nearly ran out of gas in the last quarter and only determination kept you in the game. So starting tomorrow we're going to be doing a lot more running and I'm adding a half hour of weight work to our practice. These exercises are designed to build stamina." He held up his hand and showed a space between his thumb and index finger. "This far. That's all you needed out there today to win. I'm going to make sure you get that."

Jack and I piled into the car and I turned and punched him on the shoulder and laughed. "I knew you hadn't forgotten how to play."

He grinned. "Who knew, huh?"

"You did."

He nodded. "Yeah, I did. But I gotta tell you, Cam, I never knew how much I missed playing. I love it. I love the contact and the running and the hitting." He slapped his hand on the dash. "There is nothing like it!"

It was music to my ears.

Our school has a special policy. They open the cafeteria an hour early so we can sit around and talk and have something to drink or eat and they offer a really cheap breakfast, which a surprising number of kids scarf right up.

Athletes and growing boys eat a lot and it was no big deal to pack away a second breakfast. That's what Jack and I were doing. I felt like one of Tolkien's hobbits, sitting down to "second breakfast". (Which reminds me, if you haven't read *The Lord of the Rings*, get to the library and start. They are still the most awesome books I've ever read.)

We'd had to bring our own coffee, of course, because the food police no longer allowed the school to offer coffee, or soda or much of anything really tasty. But the food is good, bacon and eggs and toast and plenty of it.

QUARRY

We had just finished eating when Mr. Canfield sat down at the table with a giant cup of Starbucks.

We smiled and said good morning and he grinned at us.

"I did some investigating," he said, "on my computer."

He looked pretty pleased with himself.

"Did you know that during Prohibition ..." He hesitated. "Do you know what Prohibition was?"

We both nodded.

"Well, it's good to know the history department is doing its job."

"It's not," Jack said. "Cam read about it."

Mr. Canfield shook his head. "What do they teach now-a-days?"

"What did you find out?" I asked.

"There was a story from a long time ago, claiming that this town had the biggest bootlegger in the state. Apparently, the guy had a huge still and he made an excellent gin, at least as good and maybe better than what was coming in from Canada, most of which came in over a lake in northern Vermont that straddles the border." He took a long swallow of coffee. I didn't know how he could drink that stuff. It's like they make it with bitter juice instead of water. "And after finding all that gin on Sunday, I began to wonder whether Mr. Batterston was involved in that."

I grinned. "We've been thinking the same thing."

"I see great minds think alike after all." He ran his hand through his thin dark hair. "But it's still pretty much of a reach to think that the bodies being dumped in the quarry are connected to that."

"Maybe after Batterston was gone," Jack said, "they remembered the quarry and when they had an extra stiff or two, it was a good place to get rid of them."

"It could be as simple as that," Mr. Canfield said. He pushed his chair back and stood up. "Let me know if you uncover anything."

"We will," I said.

I waited until he had left the cafeteria and I turned and looked at Jack. "Anything about that strike you as strange?"

He shrugged. "You mean apart from a teacher just sitting down to have a chat?"

"Yeah."

"Nope."

"Maybe I'm getting too tightly wrapped over this."

"Cam, you were born tightly wrapped."

I laughed. "Keeps things interesting."

He shook his head and grinned. "Dangerous word."

"An old Chinese curse says, 'May you live in interesting times.'" I applied myself to the plate heaped with scrambled eggs and bacon with particular vigor.

17... Dr. Batterston

At my house we eat late, usually about seven, so even with a long practice I had time to meet with Dr. Batterston. I knew from talking to him on the phone that he sounded old and perhaps a little hesitant, but I gave him no hint of what I wanted to talk about, apart from my curiosity about the quarry and his father's decision to close it down.

Every now and then in April you get a warm day that extends itself into the evening and it begins to feel a little like summer. I'm always of two minds about that. As the weather warms, trout fishing slows down, but the river has plenty of largemouth bass. The pike still hit, but usually only on cloudy days, and the stripers have headed for the saltwater which is a long way downriver.

Then, we usually take the boat to a marina near the mouth of the river and commute by car, because it's not only faster but cheaper. By then the stripers are only in the lower river and the bluefish have come back and we fish all over Long Island Sound, spending time at the Race, the Gut, Long Sand Shoals, Middle Ground, and a lot of other famous places.

I let those thoughts drift away as I walked up to the back

door. No one much uses front doors any more because driveways all go to the back of the house.

I rang the bell, and while I waited, I looked around, noting the security camera focused on me. At first, I thought that was sort of odd, but then I remembered that Dr. Batterston was in his nineties and security seemed like a good idea.

I even had time to look more closely at the house and the grounds and note that everything was in nearly perfect condition as befitted the big federal house and its position in the double row of big old houses that lined Main Street.

Finally, a voice sounded through a speaker.

"Who's there?"

"It's Cameron Bates. I called earlier?"

There was a short pause and then the door opened and I got my first look at Dr. Batterston. He was over six feet tall, slender, and he stood very straight. His face was pale, his hair white, and his eyes as blue as any I've ever seen.

"Been busy have you, Mr. Bates?"

I smiled. "Yes, sir, I have."

"Well come in, come in."

He did not offer to shake hands and instead stepped aside and closed the door.

"We'll sit in the back parlor," he said, "just follow me."

The room was more a library than a sitting room, the walls lined with books, a lot of them bound in leather. The furniture was leather too and it produced a smell I could understand.

"Sit there, if you don't mind."

I sat in a big red leather chair and watched him slowly lower himself into the chair across from me. He looked as if he were in pain and I figured it was probably arthritis.

142

QUARRY

"After you called, I asked around some and you seem to have a good reputation. To read the papers these days, one gets a different impression of our young people."

I nodded.

"You wished to talk about my father, you said."

"And the quarry. You've heard about all the bodies found up there?"

"Terrible thing. It seems somebody's been dumping them there for years."

"The divers are planning to search the rest of the quarry floor."

"That quarry was my father's particular pride. Finest granite anywhere in New England. We had been a family of farmers before my grandfather read about a need for granite in the cities and hired a man from Barre, Vermont to open up the quarry here. For two generations it was a very successful business. Then the Depression came and building stopped." He smiled. "It wasn't so very exciting, you know. Father simply closed the business and that was that."

"We've been looking around in the office," I said. "We did some forensic testing and it looks as if there may have been a gunfight there."

"With whose permission were you there?"

I lied. "The police. The whole area is a crime scene."

"Yes, yes, I suppose it is." He sat forward in his chair and frowned. "A gunfight, you say. How particularly odd. What could possibly have happened?"

"Do you know how your father died?"

He stared at me for several seconds and shook his head. "Are you always so direct?"

"I'm sorry. I've never done anything like this before."

He sat back in his chair and folded his hands in his lap, doing his best to look composed but now and then his fingers moved almost as if he had no control over them.

"My father, of course, had a heart attack."

"I read that."

"But apparently you don't think so."

"Somebody lost a lot of blood in the back office, based on the size of the stain on the floor. Whoever it was, he was probably shot with a forty-five caliber bullet, but he also managed to get off a round from his little Colt pocket auto. Apparently, he hit the guy who shot him but we think it was just a flesh wound."

"You seem surprisingly well-informed."

"We could be wrong but that's the way it looks."

"Why, if my father had been murdered, do you think we would have covered it up?"

"I guess that might depend on why he was shot."

"So it might." He smiled. "You, Mr. Bates, ought to consider going into the law."

It was a diversion and I let him divert me because the way he had dodged my questions told me that he probably knew what had happened. I was also pretty sure he wasn't going to tell me. Nobody reveals a family disgrace.

"Well, all I can say, Mr. Bates, is that I was away then, working in my first hospital after medical school, and my mother handled everything. I came home for a week to comfort mother and to help, though she was an astonishingly capable woman. But it was a terribly sad time. I think I miss him even now. He was a good man, a man who helped others, who supported his church and the town, who served on boards and even for two terms as the

QUARRY

first selectman. A man to be reckoned with."

"That's certainly what I read and what I've been told."

"True! Every bit of it!"

"From what I read, I gather the stone from the quarry was hauled down to the docks at the ferry landing and then loaded onto barges."

"It was. Exactly right. The stone went into some of the finest buildings in New York and Washington and countless other cities. It even traveled as far as San Francisco by rail. There was a railhead then in East Hartford."

"How often did they ship?"

"Why, every day. It was a very busy place."

"I wondered if, as they went deeper, they had trouble with the water."

"They did, of course, but my father hired an engineer from Providence who had particular experience with pumps and pumping and he designed special pumps that sent the water downhill to the stream. It was something to see when he turned on those pumps. Flooded the whole valley."

"Did your father have any enemies?"

"None."

"Any business partners?"

"What do you mean by partners?"

"Did he have any other businesses?"

"None that I knew of and certainly nothing that turned up when we settled the estate."

"Did you know Billy Owens?"

"I did." He crossed his legs with surprisingly little effort. "Now there was a scalawag. And together with Waverly, they cut a swath about a mile wide. The police chief spent most of his time trying to catch them breaking the law, but he was always several steps behind. Oh, they were something, those two! Traveled with bootleggers, and fast women, poached deer, gambled, oh, they were something. And then Sunday'd come and there'd be Waverly sitting there in the family pew all done up like a saint." He waved his hand as if to dismiss the past.

"Of course, after the war he came home with a chest full of medals, including the Congressional! He went to college, got a degree, got married, and raised a family, and has proven to be a fine man, the sort you point to when you want to encourage some young man who seems to think the cards have gone against him."

"And Billy Owens was reported missing in action."

"But he wasn't, you know. I saw him once at a distance, a fleeting glance, nothing more, but it was him all right."

"Do you know what happened to him?"

"I don't. Always wondered, though. He was a strange man, a loner. I think Waverly was his only friend. He was a full-blooded Pequot, one of the last I knew of. Most people treated him as a nonentity, of course, people were like that then, but if it bothered him, he never showed it."

"I heard there was a big bootlegger in town in those days."

Neither his eyes nor his general demeanor offered me any help. "Rumor is all it was. You could always get liquor here, gin mostly, and very good gin, as good or better as what came down through Canada. But that was true in a lot of places. You just had to know which door to knock on."

I grinned. "Or whether you wanted brown shoes or white shoes."

He laughed, "You have, indeed, been busy, Mr. Bates. Very

busy. I hadn't heard anyone mention that in years." He slid to the edge of the chair and a bit at a time raised himself to his feet. He looked as if it hurt. That was my signal.

I stood and followed him to the door. I could smell food cooking and I wondered if he had a cook and maybe some other servants. I should have found that out, I thought, but I couldn't see that it made any difference.

As I drove home I added up what I'd learned. It wasn't much. I still couldn't say for certain whether he knew his father had been murdered and I was even less sure that he knew anything about the bootlegging business. But then he'd spent more time away from home than here, what with private school, college, and medical school. And even if he knew, I thought it would take a mighty good lawyer to get it out of him.

I decided that after dinner I'd call Tom and see what he was up to and tell him what I had learned. I was willing to bet that very shortly there would be new locks on the doors to the office and maybe even some security people.

On the other hand, if none of that happened, it meant either that Dr. Batterston had nothing to hide, or at least wanted to appear as if that were the case.

I began to think that maybe I just didn't have enough experience reading the expressions on people's faces.

18... The cave

Practice the rest of the week, as promised, was nasty. Each day began in the weight room and then we ran windsprints until we could hardly stand and then we ran some more. The only guy who didn't seem much bothered was Jack, probably because he was in better shape that I had thought was humanly possible.

Everybody knows swimmers are strong and they have tremendous stamina, but he was ridiculous.

Coach gave us ten minutes to walk it off and recover and then we went to work, offense against defense. You can set up any defense you choose but in the end you always have to adjust to what the offense throws at you. It's why I like playing D. You have to keep your mind free and you have to concentrate on the player you're defending, constantly adjusting, trying to anticipate his next move while resisting the temptation to commit yourself too early.

And, I gotta say, we were good and getting better. But so was the offense. With Jack at point, they had changed and now the other players fed off his energy and his willingness to do whatever was necessary to get the ball into the net. He had grown

QUARRY

his whiskers to match his black, close cropped hair and he wore a black sweatband. By the end of the week he had a nickname: Black Jack.

Here I'd known this guy since my memory had begun to record things and I didn't know him at all. He laughed and he joked and he never once acted like the big dog he had become. He helped the younger guys all the time and he did it in such a way that they played better and harder and smarter. They all wanted to be just like Black Jack Waverly.

We had three days of that and then a walk-through scheduled for Saturday afternoon with a game on Sunday. I like the weekend games because more people come out to watch.

On Saturday morning Jack and I went out to the quarry, parking down by the stream where fishermen park and then cutting up through the woods. I had planned to go alone, but I couldn't get past the notion that backup might be smart.

"So what are we looking for?" he asked. "I only mention that because it might be useful."

I laughed. "I haven't got any idea," I said. "Something that doesn't belong, something that doesn't fit."

"Cam, you're the woods guy. I've hardly ever spent any time in the woods. I mean, I'm looking at trees, because that's what makes it a woods, but what else is there?"

It was a stunning admission, mostly because he had admitted to not knowing something. I stopped walking. "Look around. There are boulders here and there left by the glacier. In some places there are outcroppings of bedrock, ledges, and big overhangs that the Indians used for shelter. There are probably caves too."

"Big enough to hide a big still?"

"It could be."

"Does this go back to that idea about an underwater entrance to a cave?"

"Look, let's suppose the quarry was a front, you know, something to cover up a still? They shipped stone out of here every day. It went down to the wharf and it was loaded on boats and it went to cities up and down the East Coast. Local stuff went by truck."

"So because there was no building big enough to hold a still that size, we're looking for a cave."

"We are."

"Not to put too fine a point on this, but, ah, what are we actually looking for?"

"The back entrance. They would have had a way to escape but it would have been well hidden."

"On the Discovery Channel I saw a thing on caves. Sometimes they're in cliffs and sometimes they're just holes in the ground."

"You watch the Discovery Channel?"

"Is that so weird?"

I shook my head, remembering the homey look he'd shown for the past year and a half. "I thought maybe MTV or something, hip-hop, rap, you know."

"Junk. Never watch it. I like the Discovery Channel and the History Channel and sports."

"Awesome!"

"What else can you tell me about your theory?"

"It's a work in progress."

"Meaning you're making this up as we go."

I shrugged. "Okay. The truck traffic covered them so nobody would suspect they were shipping anything but rock. But I'm gonna guess that this must have been a pretty big operation, so they'd need a big space, and you're right. The only building was the office. I also think that a cave with a big entrance was something someone else might know about. Which raises a question. How did they get the stuff out of the cave?"

He nodded and rubbed his chin and then shook his head. "No idea. Why don't we see if we can find the cave and go from there?"

"I just thought of something else. We don't know who the sniper was."

"The camo guy?"

"Yeah. It doesn't figure that he was one of the mob guys."

"Why not?"

"I think the mafia guys figured that once all the cars had been taken out of the quarry nobody was likely to go looking for more cars so they could go on using it as long as they checked first. The sniper wanted to make sure that nobody spent any time around the quarry. I'm betting that if he'd succeeded he'd have gotten rid of the bodies and no one would have known where to look."

"You're saying that something else is going on, and when we're talking those kind of guys, these days that means drugs."

"Yeah, that's what I'm thinking."

"And what you're saying is that we could be walking right into a pack of really dangerous guys who could interfere with our ability to play on Sunday."

"Or any other day."

"So what we need to do is go home and turn this over to Tom."

"Absolutely."

He grinned. "But instead we're gonna look for that cave."

"Yeah. What the heck, we're already here and ... holy ....
I think I know how they did it. They probably ran the pumps
twenty-four hours a day so that the men could cut the granite,
and I'm gonna bet they had a road from the tunnel back to the
landing, carved right into the cliff with an area where they could
load the granite. Once the quarrymen left for the day, they loaded
up the gin."

"And if somebody came nosing around, they'd just shut off
the pumps and hide the tunnel."

I nodded. "Yeah. I think so."

"So what we're looking for is a back entrance because they'd
have to have had a way to get to the still."

"And I'm gonna guess it's not too far from where that sniper
was sitting."

"Let's go have a look."

I led the way, picking a direct route, and as we got closer I
moved very slowly, using the trees for cover and waiting and listening and staring into the woods before we moved again.

There is, I think, a lot of Bert Waverly in his grandson because Jack was into this the way he gets into a game: totally focused, alert, ready to pounce.

I cut a zigzag pattern across the hill, taking things literally one
step at a time and we climbed all the way to the top and found
nothing. So we started down the other side to the old graveyard
where we stopped so I could scratch my head and wonder why
my theory wasn't holding up.

"Kind of a weird place for a cemetery," Jack said.

I looked down at the stones, most of them fallen over now. It
was an old cemetery, a lot like the family cemeteries once found
on farms, except that it was way too large. Even stranger, there

were no names on the stones. I didn't know what, but I was pretty sure that meant something.

We walked back and forth, looking at each stone, finding nothing until we got to the cold storage enclosure, cut into the ground and buried over, with a large entrance door made of granite, not unlike the granite door to the cellar of the office. It was where they kept the bodies of people who had died in the winter when the ground was frozen. They buried them in the spring.

When I looked behind me, I realized that we were very close to the four-wheeler track and when I looked hard, I could see it through the trees, maybe fifty feet away.

I grinned at Jack and nodded and then walked up to the door and slowly pulled it open. The hinges were well oiled and it swung easily, revealing a long dark chamber.

"You going in?" Jack asked.

I pulled out the small LED flashlight I always carry and signaled him to follow. Once inside, I closed the door and then turned and started down the tunnel. It was solid granite on all sides and it led steadily downhill, turning here and there, but always heading down.

Up ahead I could hear a motor running, muffled, but still distinct, and I assumed it must be a generator. Slowly, the tunnel grew lighter and lighter and then we stepped around a corner into an enormous chamber the size of a lacrosse field with a ceiling some thirty feet above.

The floor of the chamber was covered with rows of growlights and tall marijuana plants. Far off in one corner was a great round boiler sort of affair that stood about three stories high, surrounded by a lot of copper tubing. Without question it was the still.

"Well, this is pretty much out there," Jack said.

"We need to get out of here," I said. "This place has to be wired and we probably set off an alarm somewhere."

We turned and ran back into the tunnel, and all the running we'd done in practice paid off because this was a long, long uphill run and we were blowing pretty hard by the time we got to the door. I worked the latch and pushed but nothing happened. I pushed again.

"Uh-oh," Jack said.

"Kind of a really big uh-oh." I pulled out my cell phone, expecting what I saw. No service.

"An even bigger uh-oh," Jack said.

"The question is how much time we have before they come back and make us disappear."

"I think we stand a better chance back in the marijuana room," Jack said. "More options."

I decided not to mention the Rottweilers. Surely, when they came back they'd use the dogs.

"The fact that they locked this door probably means that the water is the only other entrance," I said.

"Unless they've got divers."

"Now there's an ugly thought."

"We need to get back to the main cave fast," Jack said. "We can watch for divers and jump 'em when they come out of the water."

We ran and the fact that we were going downhill helped.

19... TRAPPED

Running pumps the blood through your system and it takes blood away from your brain which meant that by the time we got to the main cave, thinking was not an option.

Jack looked absolutely wild-eyed and I knew I looked just the same and I began walking to get my muscles relaxed, looking around, trying to figure out just how desperate our situation might be.

"You scared yet?" Jack asked.

The question stopped me. "Yeah, I think I am. We're pretty much trapped like a couple of rats and if it's the people I think it is, they've got a bunch of nasty Rottweilers."

"But you're not scared, not really."

"I'm scared. I'm just not panicked. I can still think."

"Yeah, me too. It occurs to me they may not know anything about us. They might know nothing more than that someone entered the cave and they locked us in. Now, they have to decide how to come through the door because we could be sitting here armed to the teeth waiting for them."

"I like it. I even think you're right," I said.

"I am right."

"We'll start with that. It gives us some time. I think we should blockade the tunnel. If nothing else that might keep out the dogs."

"Hard to reason with dogs."

"We also need to look for cameras."

"So they can't see what we're doing," Jack said.

We found three cameras and it was a simple enough matter to cut the wires. Some fifty feet or so back up in the tunnel the walls narrowed in. It was a good spot for a barricade and we rounded up all manner of boards and beams and tools, and bit-by-bit built a solid barricade braced with four-by-fours dug into the floor of the cave and then anchored with vertical pegs.

We walked around the cave and took stock. The old still had a chimney that ran up through the roof of the cave and now served to vent the exhaust from two big generators, one of which was running. The other apparently was used for backup. They had been placed inside the old boiler.

We also found the underwater exit, a long gradually sloping ramp that led down to the water and disappeared under the wall of the cave. It's pretty cool the way that works. The water inside the cave can only rise as high as the water outside the cave, so to keep the water from flooding the place, the tunnel from the quarry runs up hill.

"How far is it to the outside, do you think?" Jack asked.

I shrugged. "How far can you swim underwater?"

"Two hundred yards. But I swim fast, even underwater."

"I don't think I could do that."

"They've probably got a sniper up there too."

"If I were those guys, I'd certainly have that covered," I said.

QUARRY

"We could only go out after dark."

"How long would I have to hold my breath?"

"At least two minutes."

I shook my head. "Then we need to find some weapons."

Our search began turning up other things. These guys weren't just raising grass, they were making crystal meth and they had a heroin cutting operation and a place where they made crack from cocaine. This was a full-scale drug manufacturing operation.

But we found nothing beyond some boards and heavy wrenches that might double as weapons.

"We could take a bunch of the wood," Jack said, "and build a bonfire ready to light in the tunnel well back from the barricade. Cover it with green marijuana and when we lit it off, it'd fill the tunnel with smoke."

"You sure you haven't done this kind of thing before? Because that is brilliant!"

So we set that up and in the process discovered a deep, well-concealed niche in the far wall. It was full of wooden boxes, all of them holding bottles of what we discovered was gin.

"Molotov cocktails," Jack said holding up one of the bottles. "And now that I think of it, there must be gas somewhere to run the generators."

We found that soon enough; six five gallon cans, and we poured out the booze and loaded the bottles with gasoline and stuffed the tops with rags soaked in gas.

"We'll save these for when they break through the barricade," I said.

Jack reached out and picked up the end of a long garden hose that connected to the watering system for the plants.

"What's that for?"

"We can anchor this hose inside and if we have to swim for it, we'll have an air supply." He looked at me. "It'll be tricky keeping the hose shut until you need air and then getting air without letting water into the hose, but it can be done."

"Okay." I looked around. "They probably have the place rigged to explode. You gather the hose and I'll check for that."

"If it were me," Jack said, "I'd blow the roof of the cave and bury everything under tons of rock."

"But first you'd need a fire, a really hot fire, to make sure no evidence could be dug up."

What I found were five-gallon bottles of ether used in preparing heroin for market. They had been placed every twenty feet with electric wires connecting them and running back to the generator through a radio receiver. I disconnected the wires and I was holding the receiver in my hand when suddenly I felt a jolt of electric current from the leads on the receiver, let out a big yelp, and threw it into the air. Man, that took me by surprise. Not that it hurt, because it hadn't hurt anymore than an electric cattle fence, but it got my attention.

"What was that?" Jack asked.

"They pushed the button."

"Whoa ... you're saying they were just gonna waste us? These guys are really nasty."

"Do you know how close that was?"

He grinned. "Nanoseconds."

"We're a lot luckier than we have any right to expect," I said.

"Naw. Luck is something you put yourself in the way of, that's all."

"But it gives us a clue. I think we need to get out of here. Let's get that hose ready," I said.

QUARRY

"What do you know that you haven't told me?"

"They'll have covered the chimney. It'll take awhile but with no outlet the carbon monoxide from the generator is gonna start building up. If we shut it off we're in the dark and that makes things a whole lot harder."

We unhitched the hoses, stretched them out, screwed them back together, and coiled them carefully. We had at least four hundred feet. Jack came up with a big locking pliers to seal the end of the hose.

"If there's a sniper," I said, "he's on the far side of the quarry. We need enough hose to get to that side underwater where he won't be able to get a shot at us."

"Keep thinking, Cam, keep thinking."

"I also think we ought to preserve the evidence. Let's move all the ether jugs into the tunnel. If they come in, we wait until they reach the barricade, then set it off and swim out. All that stuff going off at once oughta roast them to a crisp."

"Man, you've got a truly criminal mind. I like that."

It took us about fifteen minutes or so to set up all the five-gallon glass jugs and two rows of our Molotov cocktails in the tunnel by the barricade and it was an impressive array of explosive power.

"What if someone comes looking for us?" Jack asked. "They could walk right into this."

"Kind of complicates things, doesn't it," I said.

He pointed to the exit. "This may not be as bad as I first thought. The water is about five feet below the top of the tunnel out to the quarry. If the drop is shallow enough in the tunnel we may have air at the top of the tunnel for a long way."

And that made me feel a whole lot better.

We heard a crash from above as the door flew open and we could hear the dogs coming and we poured a fair amount of gas on the jugs and then ran a trail of gas down to the icy water.

"You're trapped!" someone shouted. "There's no other way out of here. Give yourselves up and we'll let you go!"

I lit a match and dropped it into the gas and watched it run along the wall, out of sight from the tunnel and we waded into the water and swam the ten feet to the tunnel.

Jack had been right about the gap between the water the roof, but we ducked under the water just in case the blast came close. The explosion was so fierce that it lit up the water and shook the walls. We pulled out hose and swam for freedom.

In the movies I've seen people swimming out of underwater passages and it always makes my hands sweat. I have a mortal fear of drowning.

Jack surfaced, reached down, and pulled me up into the air. The space was only a couple of feet but it was plenty and we swam steadily, turned onto our backs so we could breath.

And then the space ended and we ducked under the water and swam breast stroke. I couldn't have gone more than a minute before I tugged on Jack's coat and he stopped and handed me the air hose. Now, we had to go by feel and I got the hose into my mouth and took a long deep breath.

It was so dark I couldn't tell up from down, except that when I stopped swimming I felt myself begin to sink and that got me oriented. I like gravity a lot. It has all kinds of practical uses.

It seemed to take forever but each time I began to run out of air, Jack handed me the hose. The air tasted of the fire inside the cave. Just as I had begun to give up hope of ever reaching the end, it began to grow lighter. Jack made us drop to the floor of

QUARRY

the tunnel and we swam out into the quarry and floated upward to have a look. The sniper was right where I thought he would be and we were just lucky that he was looking up toward the top of the hill above the cave.

We dropped out of sight and began swimming across. I had no idea how deep we were, but when I looked down I couldn't see the bottom. We might have been half-way across when the air hose came up short. We both inhaled as much of the air as we could and then let go of the hose and swam and swam and swam and I was nearly out of air when Jack took my arm and we swam up toward the surface, a glistening mirror above.

We burst out of the water near the wall of the cliff on the far side and I was panting and hanging onto the rock. Jack wasn't even breathing hard. But then he was in his element. I think he must have some otter genes.

Up for air.

He pointed across to the other side and we could see a huge column of smoke rushing skyward. In the distance we could hear sirens and I wondered how long the sniper would sit there. A single shot answered my question as the guy tumbled over the edge and plunged into the quarry.

Then we began to swim toward the landing. I watched Jack vault himself out of the water to a standing position on the ledge and then Tom reached down, took my hand, and dragged me up onto solid ground.

"You guys have gotta stop doing stuff like this," Tom said. "It could get you killed."

I looked at him and then at Jack and rolled onto my back and laughed and Jack laughed with me.

Tom waited for us to calm down and, finally, I sat up, rolled onto my knees and stood. "You remember asking me to tell you if I found any drugs?"

He nodded.

"Wait 'til you see what's inside that hill."

Tom grinned. "You got time to tell me what happened?"

I looked at my watch. "We got practice in about an hour."

"Just get me started."

We did that, taking turns, and when Tom had heard enough, he took out his cell phone, wandered away to where we couldn't hear and began making calls.

Both of us stripped down, wrung the water out of our clothes, put them back on, and lay down in the warm sun.

"I can hardly believe we did that," Jack said. "It all seems like a dream."

"More like a nightmare where you wake up soaked in sweat."

"You got that right."

QUARRY

Tom was still on the phone when two big Blackhawk choppers popped over the hill and, flying right at treetop height, shot past and over the next hill, probably headed for the house.

"Whoa, was that awesome or what!" Jack said.

"That was the DEA," Tom said.

"They got here kind of fast, didn't they?" I asked.

"They've got a unit at Brainard and they're on full alert."

"They've got their own air force?" I asked.

Tom grinned. "Beats sitting in traffic."

That was all we saw of the police mop-up. Not until later did we learn that they had arrested six people and found the toasted bodies of two dogs and four men in the tunnel. Everything in the cave survived.

The media called it the single biggest drug factory ever taken down and no one mentioned our names because that would have been like waving a red flag in the face of the people connected to the guys we'd done in. Even so, I hoped those guys would spend a long, long time in prison because with what had already happened, they might have tracked us down pretty quickly.

We got to practice on time, and luckily it was just a walk-through. I don't think either of us could have handled a normal practice. Even the walk-through was almost too much and I noticed Coach watching us closely.

I went home, ate dinner and went up to bed. I slept like a rock: no nightmares, no memories of even having been asleep and I woke in the morning at about eight, alert and ready to play.

I came downstairs to find everyone gathered in the kitchen, with Mom busy cooking up a big feed of pancakes and sausages. I don't think I had ever been so hungry.

While I was eating, Dad began. "After you went to bed, Tom dropped by to fill us in on your activities."

"Kind of a strange day," I said.

"Did you really do all that?" Lance asked.

I nodded. "It was more like accidental. We were just looking for the cave and got trapped."

And, then, for the first time since I could remember, Mom began to act like a mother. "How could you have taken such a risk? Do you know how stupid that was?"

"I know it was stupid, Mom. But we had no idea we were in any trouble until we got into the main room of the cave and the place was filled with marijuana plants. We were looking for Batterston's old still. I mean, well, we had no idea that there was anything more than that down there."

That wasn't enough for her and that was okay. I'd had a pretty free rein for a long time and I thought maybe if I were in her position, I'd have been a little upset too.

Dad, on the other hand, seemed hardly ruffled. "Tom said something about using garden hoses to supply you with air on the swim out."

"That was Jack's idea. Man, he is absolutely fearless. He can swim underwater for two minutes, but I needed to have air."

It's the way it works in a thing like that. Moms get terror stricken and dads just shake their heads and thank God that somehow you survived and because you did survive, well, it makes them pretty proud of their sons.

My job was just to answer questions until they stopped coming, never showing the least irritation and always admitting to being significantly stupid. Lance helped out.

"You couldn't have known it was dangerous. And once you

QUARRY

were there, they couldn't have left any witnesses."

"The whole place was set to blow," I said. "They had five-gallon jugs of ether among the plants all wired to go off. But we found that and traced the wire and unhooked it and I was holding the receiver when the signal came and it was like holding onto an electric fence."

"Awesome, absolutely awesome," Lance said.

"Lance," Dad said, "remember what Tom said last night. This stays here. It does not go outside this house. These guys had to have been connected and the guys they were connected to are pretty unhappy just now and will be for a long time to come."

"I'm not stupid, you know."

I had to repeat the whole story from start to finish, filling in details Tom had either left out or stuff we hadn't remembered to tell him. In the end, even Mom was impressed and I think I was too, having suddenly understood just how close we'd come to being piles of ashes on the cave floor. Mostly I remembered being underwater in the tunnel and running out of air and that's a feeling I never want to have again.

20... BLACK JACK

The game was our second in a row against a top-ranked team and Coach made it clear in the locker room that we needed to win this one.

"I wouldn't make a demand like this unless I thought you could pull it off. What I know is that you can. You guys have the talent and the chemistry. You play as a team. All you have to do is play the way you played on Tuesday and we end up as one of the teams in this state to be reckoned with."

He stood with his arms folded across his chest. "We discussed our game plan yesterday and nothing has changed. Our first goal is a four-goal lead in the first quarter. Our next goal is to increase that by two in the following quarter so we're up by six at the half. Our next goal is to increase that by four in the third quarter. Our final goal is a win."

The thing was, however improbable that might have sounded, every guy in the room knew we could do it. We had not a single doubt. I knew the defense could hold them and I knew that Jack was gonna take his game to yet another level.

But North Haven was no pushover, they were strong and fast

and well-coached. What gave us the initial edge was playing at home in front of a surprisingly large crowd, or at least that helped the younger guys. I don't think Jack ever heard them and I know I didn't.

They got the ball first and attacked and I attacked back, coming up on the wingman who had the ball and riding him hard, forcing him farther and farther toward the edge of the field, giving him no lane to pass so that when he got rid of the ball he just sort of tossed it back toward his defensive guys and he got nothing on it, just a soft high lob, and Jack came out of nowhere, leaped and stole the pass and hit the ground running at full speed.

I knew and everyone on our team knew what he had in mind, and the defense had no chance. He ran faster, dodging, faking, leaving guys standing there trying to figure out how he could've gotten past them and then with one last fake and spin he stepped past the last defender into the open and the goalie never had a chance as Jack faked at the left corner of the goal and then flipped his stick with his wrists and shot the ball into the right corner.

Suddenly the guys on the bench jumped up and started chanting BLACK JACK! BLACK JACK! BLACK JACK! Then the crowd took it up and the guys from North Haven began sneaking looks at Jack, grinning back at them like a hungry pirate, who really enjoyed his work.

I grinned to myself, knowing that the coach at Johns Hopkins was gonna get a call from Dad. He'd already sent them my videos.

The shock of that goal and the chanting seemed to take the wind out of North Haven and that lasted for most of the first period, during which we scored four more times and gave them nothing, not because our defense was all that great, but because they just couldn't pull it together. We'd gotten into their heads with that first goal and it made them think that maybe our one goal loss to Cheshire hadn't been the fluke they'd been told.

The next quarter got a little screwy. They had really begun to fall apart, but they turned it into a zoo and it was surprisingly effective in the way it rattled our offense, with the exception of Jack who scored three more goals. They got nothing.

We had beaten our first half goal but Coach was not handing out congratulations. Instead, he lit into what we could have done better. Hey, this is lacrosse we're talking here. You let up for an instant and you're yesterday's lunch. Everyone of us liked praise but that comes after the last whistle when you can put the game in the bank.

Those of us who had been around a while knew that praise can get in your way. Your head swells up like a summer watermelon and you begin to think that you deserve to win and that makes it certain that you'll lose. So Jack, C-Shack, and I made sure every word Coach said got through to those rookies. We made them understand that when your coach tells you what to do you do it, unless maybe it's crossword puzzles.

Besides, he was right and when you know that you can take what he says onto the field and concentrate on strategy and tactics and let the rest take care of itself. What I mean, is that some things you have to think about and others have to happen by instinct. When you shoot at a goal, if you think about the target, if you aim, you'll miss. If you just shoot, you have a better chance of scoring.

When it came to criticism, the defense got a free ride. |But hey, we were working on a shutout. What Coach wanted, what had to happen now, was for the rest of the offense to step it up,

QUARRY

because the fact was that Jack had scored all eight goals. A swarming defense can stop one player.

"From here on," Coach said, "Jack is going to be double- and triple-teamed. Every time he takes a pass, they're gonna smother him and that means people are going to be open. What I'm looking for are crossing moves in front of the goal to screen the third man up, then I want the crossers to set screens to give him an open shot at the goal. My bet is that even if we score, they are not gonna let Jack out of jail. But if we score enough, they're gonna have to back off."

He looked around at us, staring into each man's eyes, waiting and then moving on and then he held up his hand, balled it into a fist and held it out toward us. He didn't shout, he just pumped that fist once. "Okay. Let's go get 'em!"

We rushed onto the field ready to attack, certain we were invincible, all of us feeling as fresh as if we starting the first half instead of the second.

Nasty, nasty, nasty, the game turned into a free-for-all. They came out swinging and slashing and fighting and sure enough they double- and triple-teamed Jack and it left them totally vulnerable. We scored twice in three minutes and then their coach chose to resort to a more defensive game, looking for breakaways to try to get back into it.

Maybe against somebody else's defense that might have worked. But we covered the guys trying to sneak in behind us and nobody got open.

On one play they tried a long pass and I timed it just right, leaped, picked it off, and while I was still in the air I fired a lead pass to Jack who simply blew past the two guys guarding him, slashing right between them. And when the other defenders mobbed him at the goal, he tucked his stick in close, dove to the ground at full speed, rolled under them, back up onto his feet, and faked out the goalie so thoroughly that all he had to do was toss the ball into the goal.

Cam makes a great pass.

When the game ended we were up fifteen to zip. A shutout! And I knew without the least doubt that I was gonna graduate a winner. Well, that's not exactly true. You never know that. You just know you have a chance and then you work your butt off and you never, ever let up. It's a total rush. It makes you dizzy at times.

Not until the game was over and we were picking up our gear

and heading for the locker room did I happen to glance at the stands and there was Jack's grandfather, standing beside a man his age, a man of medium height, with long flowing white hair and dark eyes. What caught my eye was the way he stood, his back as straight as an arrow. Then Jack grabbed my arm and we walked toward the two men.

"Well, well," Jack's grandfather said, "now that was a demonstration!" He turned to the man next to him. "I'd like you both to meet an old friend of mine, whom I recently discovered is alive and well and living not so very far away. Jack, Cam, this is Billy Owens, or, as he's known now, Billy Red Eagle. He's a Pequot tribal shaman."

We shook hands and he smiled and nodded each time, and he missed nothing, even the question I asked with my eyes.

"We're having dinner at my house this evening."

"Who's doing the cooking?" Jack asked.

"Your mother's helping because your grandmother's arthritis has been acting up again. Billy has a driver these days and he has some things to tell you that might be of interest; in fact, I think I can guarantee that. So you boys get over to the house at about seven. Things should be ready by then."

It was an order and somehow Mr. Waverly had a way of making you understand that he expected you to obey. Not that it mattered. Nothing could have kept me away. Not often do you get to have dinner with a legend, let alone two.

I grinned. "Does this mean that Jack's mother knows about lacrosse?"

Mr. Waverly smiled. "She was cheering louder than anyone here."

I nodded. "So was I. Did you see that first goal?" I reached over and punched Jack on the shoulder. "The big guy's the best," I said.

Jack laughed. "And you pitched a shutout on defense. Nobody does that in lacrosse. And what about that pass? You threw it while you were still in the air! Man! Bates to Waverly and into the goal!"

Billy Owens grinned. "I like the name: Blackjack."

Well why wouldn't he? They made a lot of money on blackjack at his casino.

Afterward, at home, after my family gave me a hero's welcome, and then later, when I had a few moments alone in my room, I began to draw parallels between my friendship with Jack and his grandfather's friendship with Billy Owens. They acted like they knew each other's minds and after the past two days, my friendship with Jack had reached a similar level. I also noted that the entire time we had stood there, Billy Owens had said only those few words and yet I had come away feeling as if we'd had a long conversation. I wasn't at all sure what to make of that.

21...Red Eagle Speaks

Mrs. Waverly, Jack's grandmother, answered the door and she took me by surprise because she looked a good deal younger than her husband. It was something I should have known, but I simply didn't.

She welcomed us with a warm smile, a big hug for Jack and one for me. Then she stepped back and looked at us both. "I'm not sure what to make of you two."

Jack shrugged. "Right time, right place, right tools."

"Might have been a little lucky too," I said. "But not in the game. No luck there. Just Black Jack Waverly doing what he does."

She laughed and shook her head and she looked at her grandson as if she had never seen him before. It happens. Guys grow up and it always takes the adults by surprise.

"Well," she said, "let's go join the old guys." She had wonderfully sharp, clear blue eyes and her gray hair was pulled back into a bun and she was slender and tall and stood very straight.

"Would you like something to drink?" she asked as she led us toward the living room. "I have plenty of cold Coke. Around here that's a must. Bert drinks almost a case a week, despite his doctor's warning."

Mr. Waverly and Billy Owens sat in the leather chairs on either side of the fireplace, where the bright flames beat back the chill of a spring evening.

"Come in, come in," Mr. Waverly said. "Glad you could make it."

The greeting, especially since one of us was his grandson, seemed oddly detached.

Mrs. Waverly went for the Cokes and we sat on the couch, facing the fire.

I had never met a full-blooded Indian until today and now, looking at him in the dancing light of the fire, I imagined how he would have looked in native clothing around an open fire in the middle of a tribal compound. I also thought it was pretty cool that my favorite sport had been invented by American Indians.

"From what Jack told me," Mr. Waverly said, "you discovered the great secret of the Batterstons."

"We did," I said. "The still is there even now, and we also found about fifty cases of gin."

"It was very good gin," Billy Owens said. "I know because I was the distiller." He waited for us to get past our surprise, then frowned and shook his head, his long gray hair swishing back and forth. "But I never disliked a man more than Batterston. Oh, he was fair with his workers and he paid them well enough, but he acted like he was king of the world, you see. He never spoke to me because I was an Indian, or at least I thought that was what was behind it." He shook his head. "I don't suppose you can ever know a thing like that for sure, and I'm no psychologist. On the other hand he was in a terrible spot. I made the gin so he had to be careful, not so much because I would turn him in but because the men he sold the gin to wouldn't have tolerated an interruption in their supply.

"As long as he supplied the gin he was safe. But if that broke down, then they'd kill him so he couldn't rat them out to the cops."

That piece of information provided a lot of people with a motive to have shot Mr. Batterston and I filed it away.

"Did any of the men in the quarry know what was going on?" I asked.

He shrugged. "Well, they knew he was up to something, but they didn't know what. Everything came and went in sealed boxes and barrels. Each day a crew from Providence came in and loaded and unloaded the cave. The quarrymen were gone for the day by then, but they suspected.

"All the gin I made was sold to the gang from Providence that supplied our night workers, and for perhaps five years I ran that still day and night. I had two helpers, both Indians, and the money kept us very quiet. We put it in the bank and never touched it. We almost never left the cave and when we did it was by the back entrance in the cemetery."

"And nobody went to the police," I said.

He nodded. "We humanized Batterston. I made him raise the salaries of every employee and put the extra money into bank accounts scattered from Hartford to New London. Now, I would like to hear the story of how you found the entrance and what happened in my cave."

Jack and I took turns, his grandfather and Billy Owens nodding now and then and smiling here and there.

"What we haven't solved is the murder of Mr. Batterston."

Mr. Waverly looked over at his old friend. "I believe Billy might be some help along those lines."

He looked at us for some time, his dark eyes absorbing every detail. Then he seemed to straighten in the chair. "I did it," he said. "Shot him with his own gun after I took it away from him and he shot me." He picked up a coffee mug from the table next to him and took a long swallow. "Prohibition was over but the Depression was in full swing. The demand for liquor was high and I got an idea that I could get a license and start up the old still again. But this time everything would be legal. So I went up to meet him at the office and things went bad right from the start.

"He told me he wouldn't do it because they would have to send in government inspectors and they'd figure out pretty quick that the still had been there for a long time and must have been a bootlegging operation. So I offered to move everything out of the cave and down to the reservation and apply for a license." He grinned. "And I don't want to hear any bad jokes here about Indians and firewater."

We all laughed.

"But he wouldn't even agree to that. Well, that made no sense at all to me and I thought maybe he still had something going with the Providence crooks. Until you lived through those times, it's hard to understand how desperate we were. All over the country men were on the road looking for work of any kind. They left their families behind and hit the road, riding on trains in empty boxcars, hitchhiking, doing whatever they could. Some of them were just drifting, lost souls, men with no future, denied the one thing they knew how to do: work and take care of their families. In household after household wives would wake up in the morning to find their husbands had gone. Sometimes they left notes,

QUARRY

sometimes they simply disappeared and were never heard from again.

"It began to happen here too. Most simply saw it as a sign of the times and they pushed on, clinging to hope. But when the men who had worked at the quarry began to disappear, I took notice. They'd all had substantial bank accounts and they should have been able to weather things through. They wouldn't have been able to live high on the hog, exactly, but they would have survived until the economy picked up and people went back to work.

"But it was mostly rumor because I had moved down to North Stonington to live with my people on the reservation, such as it was. The money I had saved, I used to make life better for everyone but it was running out." He shook his head. "The rumors grew, and finally I came back and asked around and very shortly discovered that only three of us were left out of the people who had worked at the quarry, just me and my two assistants who had gone back to New York to live with the Senecas, their people.

"I got in touch with Batterston and told him I'd like to meet him in the office at the quarry. I told him I wanted to talk some more about buying the still from him. I told him that I had cleared it with the elders in the Tribe and that it would be our salvation. Well, I had been pretty certain he wouldn't want to see me, but he agreed and I wondered if he saw it as an opportunity to get rid of any evidence of what had gone on at the quarry and had been the source of his money."

He took another swallow of his coffee. "But that wasn't at all what he had in mind. He was sitting at his desk when I walked in and without a single word he pulled that big Colt from under his desk and I rushed him, knocked him from his chair, took the gun

177

away, and stood there pointing the gun at him. He was lying on his right side and he kept his eyes on me as he sat up.

"'Stay where you are,' I said. And he sat with his left side facing me, perhaps seven or eight feet away, his head turned toward me. Not even in the war did I see such fear in a man's eyes.

" 'You killed them all,' I said."

" 'There's no proof of that,' he answered.

"'And if you killed me that was one more out of the way. Where are the bodies? In the quarry?'

"He knew then that he was done. Either I would kill him or I would go to the police. Desperate men resort to desperate measures and he suddenly pulled out the pocket Colt, but I turned, and even at close range small pistols are hard to shoot. The bullet passed through the flesh on my left shoulder and I pulled up the Colt and shot him in the head before he could get off another round. The gun is at the bottom of the quarry.

"What I told you before about finding the body wasn't exactly true," Mr. Waverly said. "I went there to look for the safe. I needed money for my family. Instead I found the body and the safe open and empty."

"I emptied it," Billy Owens said. "There was almost ten thousand in cash. I went back to the reservation and waited for the news but when it came I was surprised to find that the cause of death was listed as a heart attack."

"Which meant," Mr. Waverly said, "that either someone in the family knew about the still and didn't want the police up there looking around, or they couldn't stand the shame."

I thought of Dr. Batterston sitting in the big old house and I wondered if he had known. His mother and perhaps a family lawyer would have been in control.

QUARRY

"What does it mean to be a shaman?" I asked.

He smiled. "Purely honorary these days. I sit on the board and I advise. I am treated well, very well, as I am the only full-blooded Pequot anyone in the tribe has known. Some think there is great magic I can bring. I find that useful."

Mr. Waverly laughed. "People are prone to believe that age brings wisdom, though what it really does is make you more cautious. In its own way that is a sort of wisdom."

"Especially," Billy Owens said, "if you try to look like one of those old photographs of Crazy Horse or Sitting Bull." He laughed. "In the end, we are all just men, doing the things that men do and trying to do them well. There are no differences between men of different races, there are only differences between men and women."

Well, that one took me by surprise. All I'd heard in school was that males and females were exactly alike, except that boys were too aggressive and noisy and physical. I didn't think the feminists were gonna get on board with that idea, but the truth is, I didn't care whether they did or not. We are what we are and from Billy Owens I had just learned that such things cannot be changed.

I had also just learned something else. I thought about my talk with Dr. Batterston and the pinched barren look in his eyes. He had lived with the fear of discovery his whole life and it had been a terrible weight. And now it was going to come out. The still had been discovered and there would be questions and times had changed. The family would no longer be able to control the information and silence their critics.

And yet, he could deny having known anything about what had gone on at the quarry. He had been away at school then and I thought most people would believe the sons were blameless.

Jack looked over at Billy Owens. "How did you manage to disappear?"

"I had nothing to do with it. The War Department took care of that. I was in Germany and they decided to rotate me back home and when I got here they had lost the records. I no longer existed. I just walked away and then later someone found the records. By then I was back on the reservation and they couldn't find me. They closed the file by stamping on it, 'missing in action.'"

He sat up in his chair. "What I'd like to know is when you're playing next. Watching you today, watching the way you played, took me back to the stories I heard about lacrosse. Perhaps we can build a lacrosse academy on the reservation as a means of celebrating our contribution."

Mr. Waverly grinned. "Don't make it sound like it was the only contribution, Billy. Every boy in America for hundreds of years has grown up with images of Indians in his mind. We see them as warriors, and we wish in many ways we could be like them. It has conditioned the way this country grew and it continues to do that. I suspect it's why the movie people always find ways to get them into pictures."

It was true. We had always played cowboys and Indians when we were little kids and I still loved westerns better than any other kind of movie. But what I liked best was Indian lore and legends. Don't get me wrong here. History is about conquest and whether it's moral or not doesn't mean anything. It's just what humans do. No one either surrenders or occupies territory without a fight.

Still, there was a magic to Indian warriors. They were courageous and tough. It's the kind of symbol you want for your team and I liked it a lot that we were called the Tomahawks. And I had always been proud of being part Pequot.

"Mr. Owens," I asked, "could you supply our team with a true Pequot pattern that could be made into sweatbands for us all to wear?"

He looked at me, weighing carefully what he saw.

"I mean we're not called the Tomahawks for nothing. And maybe it would be a way to honor the Pequots who held this land before we did."

He nodded his head and smiled. "I will see to it."

Mr. Waverly laughed and turned to Billy. "This young man is part Pequot."

Billy nodded. "I know," he said. "From his great grandmother, a woman with particular powers. She had an ability to know what was going to happen before it did."

"Awesome!" Jack said to me. "You do that all that time."

22... ODDS AND ENDS

Monday morning I called Tom and met him at the station on my way to school.

We sat in his office and he was looking pretty happy.

"What can I do for you, Cam?"

"It's about Dr. Batterston."

"You mean, are we going after him?"

"Yeah."

He shook his head. "Even if we had any way to connect him to the bootlegging operation, the statute of limitations expired a long, long time ago."

"So you're not."

"No. The marijuana operation is the focus here. We're already getting calls and now it looks like we may have shut down the main source of income for the guys in Providence. You guys did an absolutely phenomenal job."

"It was really just an accident."

"Maybe, but you saved all the evidence and wiped out a bunch of guys with records that should've gotten them put away for life a long time ago. Pretty good day's work, I think."

QUARRY

I grinned. "What's gonna happen to the quarry and the cave?"

"It belongs to Dr. Batterston. He has sole title. I haven't talked to him beyond telling him about what happened there."

"All it said in the news was that he owned the quarry."

Tom grinned. "The DEA agents talked to him and as far as they're concerned he wasn't involved."

"Did they ask him about the still?"

"They thought it was a furnace to keep the temperature up in the cave for growing the marijuana." He laughed.

"Wow. They really didn't know what it was?"

"Nope." He looked at me, his head cocked to the side. "What have you got in mind here?"

"I thought I would go talk to Dr. Batterston," I said.

"Why?"

"Just to let him know that no one is talking about the old still."

"Nobody even cares."

"But he would. It would raise questions about his father."

"Which we can't prove."

"Actually, I can."

"What?"

"Billy Owens was his distiller."

"Billy Owens? The Indian? He's alive?"

"I met him last night at Mr. Waverly's. He's a Pequot shaman now."

"Does he know what happened in the office?"

"He does."

Tom looked at me carefully and then smiled and shook his head. "You do get around, don't you?"

"There were no witnesses."

"So no way to connect him with the murder."

"It was self-defense."

"Batterston shot first?"

"He did."

"I think that supports what Mr. Canfield said. Case closed."

"I was hoping you'd see it that way."

I called on Dr. Batterston after practice and we sat in his library in big old brown leather chairs. He looked older than when I had seen him last and I wondered if he'd been given some bad news.

"Well," he said, his voice sounding oddly scratchy, "what have you come to tell me."

"A story about your father."

"I suspected as much."

I began the story and as I talked, I could see the permanent frown lines in his face relax. Several times he rubbed his face and each time he looked younger. When I finished, he sat for perhaps a minute or longer and then he drew a deep breath and smiled.

"Finally, it's over. You can't imagine what a relief it is to know what really happened. This thing has been like a crown of thorns and now it's gone."

I smiled back at him. "I'm glad you see it that way."

"I always suspected something odd had been going on, but I never knew about the bootlegging or the cave. It also explains a hole in my father's papers that I never understood. What wealth he had was mostly wiped out in the crash. Oh, there was enough left to have lived on and for two or three years the quarry still brought in money but no where near what it had before the crash.

QUARRY

Yet when he died, he left an enormous estate. My brother and I have puzzled over that all these years, trying to guess at what he had done but nothing ever turned up. Perhaps if we had known he'd been shot in a gunfight, it would have led us in the right direction." He smiled. "Perhaps we never wanted to know. Perhaps we suspected that it would leave a permanent stain on the family and we did, after all, have children." He sighed deeply and then frowned. "Is there any need for this to come out now?"

"None. I checked with the authorities. The statute of limitations has expired. The shooting was self-defense and it's not going to appear in the files. There's no need. The records will stay as they are."

"It would seem to me that I owe you a substantial debt."

I shook my head slowly. "There's no debt. Jack and I have been paid in experience and knowledge." I grinned. "Besides it was also one heck of an adventure."

For the first time, his smile was open and genuine. "You will, Mr. Cameron Bates, go a long, long way."

I knew it was fine compliment, but I also knew it would take some time to figure out exactly what he had meant.

"I have one thing to ask," he said. "I should like to have you show me that cave."

"It's a bit of a walk."

"Oh, I may look old, but I walk two miles a day. Not fast, mind you, but I get it done. How rough is the ground?"

"There's a path."

"Perhaps this coming weekend, if the weather's good."

"I'll call."

"Good. Good. I think that seeing it all will be the final step in putting it to rest. I just wish my brother were alive. He was more tortured than I." Suddenly he looked up. "I might even take in a lacrosse game. I hear that you and Bert Waverly's grandson are on a tear."

"You might see Billy Owens there."

"I think I should like to see him. I think, in the end, that my family owes him a tremendous apology for the way my father treated him, not to mention the others who worked for him. And once I've seen the cave, I think I'll sell the property."

"You might call my dad, if you do that."

"You think he would be interested?"

"I'm pretty sure he would."

It was just a guess, but a good one. Dad bought the property and then hired divers to come in and they found the remains of the men who had worked the quarry.

What none of the experts found were the cases of gin in the obscure niche in the back of the cave. After Dad had gotten someone to test it, I gave a case to Billy and Mr. Waverly and Dr. Batterston.

That same evening Dad mixed himself a martini (shaken and not stirred) and declared that it was the best gin he'd ever tasted.

Of course I wanted to try it, but hey, I wasn't old enough and Dad is a stickler about the law, even at home. But the way I looked at it, there was a lot of gin in that cave and I guessed it would most likely last until I got to twenty-one.

As it turned out, that gin, or at least gin made on Billy Owen's formula would be available for a long time to come. The Pequots decided, after a tasting session or two, that there was money to be made and they set about building a plant on the reservation to make Red Eagle Gin. They left the old equipment in the cave because they were building a state of the art distillery.

Later I even found out what happened to the fish in the stream. The drug factory guys had been dumping chemicals into the brook. Luckily everything was water soluble and it had washed away. The state came in and tested the water and the bottom sediments and decided it was safe to restock.

I got the lacrosse team to help and, using stocking floats, we released trout for two miles up the stream. It was a wild day, with most everyone managing to get soaked to the bone.

You probably won't believe this, but not a single guy on the team had ever done any serious fishing. We lived along one of the best fishing rivers in the East, a river with good enough water to support Great Northern Pike, a fish that does not survive in anything but very clean water, and all they'd done was fish for some bluegills when they were little kids.

Meanwhile, our lacrosse season played out the way we had taken it. We finished with a winning season and we were ranked third in the state. So Jack and I went out playing on a winning team.

What's more, Johns Hopkins had found room for Jack in September. I'd already been accepted, but once Dad drove down there with the films of Jack and they checked his SATs, and his times in the pool, he was in. Sometimes things just work out ... but not without a substantial amount of butt busting.

My next job was to make sure Jack stayed in school. He's smart enough, even at a school like Johns Hopkins, but he was gonna be swimming and playing lacrosse and one varsity sport is enough to bury a lot of guys.

What I wanted to bury were schools like Syracuse, Duke, Army, and Virginia. Never hurts to have goals ... and when it comes to lacrosse, the more the better.

In June, the Tribe began construction of the lacrosse field and training facility. They named it in honor of a quirky, driven kid who was part Indian ... me ... Cameron Bates.

Don't ever let anyone ever tell you that hard work doesn't pay off.